4/05   # 2

D0399288

STEVE + CARO

TO LOTS OF SUCCESS AND FULFILLMENT OF YOUR DREAMS.

what people are saying about *deliberate success*

"Success is a deliberate and principle-centered journey. This book will assist you in successfully moving from where you are to where you want to be."

—Stephen Covey, Ph.D.
Author of *The 7 Habits of Highly Effective People*

"*Deliberate Success* will engage you in an important journey of taking control of your destiny, empowering your teams, and creating an even more fulfilling life."

—Brian Tracy
President, Brian Tracy International

"If you want a fresh perspective on leadership principles that will help your organization stand the test of time, read this book."

—Ken Blanchard, Ph.D.
Coauthor of *The One-Minute Manager* and *Leadership by the Book*

"This powerful book will position you for winning in business and in life through principles and tools that transcend time."

—Denis Waitley, Ph.D.
Author of *Psychology of Winning*

"*Deliberate Success* will challenge and inspire you to be your best while providing pragmatic tools that make a good leader great. It's a must for any leader to read!"

—Colleen Barrett
President & COO, Southwest Airlines

"*Deliberate Success* contains an enormous amount of information that will help you to attain and sustain your personal best."

—Richard Thalheimer
CEO, Chairman & Founder, The Sharper Image

"This compelling book provides great tools for turning your business dreams into reality and in experiencing more of what you are seeking in life."

—Jack Daughery
President, International Leadership Development, Inc.

deliberate success

realize your vision
with purpose, passion, and performance

by
eric allenbaugh, ph.d.

CAREER
PRESS

Franklin Lakes, NJ

Deliberate Success
Edited by Jodi L. Brandon
Typeset by John J. O'Sullivan
Cover design by Cheryl Cohan Finbow
Printed in the U.S.A. by Book-mart Press

To order this title, please call toll-free 1-800-CAREER-1 (NJ and Canada: 201-848-0310) to order using VISA or MasterCard, or for further information on books from Career Press.

The Career Press, Inc., 3 Tice Road, PO Box 687,
Franklin Lakes, NJ 07417
www.careerpress.com

Library of Congress Cataloging-in-Publication Data

Allenbaugh, Eric.
    Deliberate success : realize your vision with purpose, passion, and performance / by
    Eric Allenbaugh.
        p. cm.
    Includes bibliographical references and index.
    ISBN 1-56414-617-0 (cloth)
    1. Success in business. 2. Success—Psychological aspects. I. Title.
HF5386 .A5434 2002
650.1—dc21   2001059877

dedication

*With love and appreciation, I gratefully dedicate this book
to my wife, my cheerleader, my lifelong partner,
and my best friend—Kay Allenbaugh.*

acknowledgments

Many people have touched my life in both my personal and professional journey, some who I cannot even call by name. Several individuals, however, deserve special thanks for their contribution to the creation of *Deliberate Success: Realize Your Vision With Purpose, Passion, and Performance.* This book could not have been written without their support and influence.

- Special thanks goes to Kay, my wife, for her ongoing support, encouragement, and spirited energy.
- Thanks to my late Dad, who continues to be a positive force and inspiration in my life.
- Thanks to my sons for their wonderful contributions to my life and to my learning.
- Thanks to Denis Waitley for his gracious support and for his contribution of the "Foreword" to *Deliberate Success*.
- Thanks to Ruthita Fike, Michael Jackson, Steve Ervin, and many other clients—who I am proud to call close friends—for encouraging me to commit these principles and tools to writing.
- Thanks to Dan and Cindy Potter, Jim and Jan Hibbard, and Scott Miller and Jody Miller Stevenson for keeping the vision of this book.

- Thanks to the leaders and consultants who have contributed some of their best thinking in the form of "Deliberate Success Gems" included throughout this book.
- Thanks to my clients, who have been a rich source of learning and discovery for me—and thanks for their referrals.
- Thanks to the consultants and authors who have inspired and influenced me.
- Thanks to the many other friends and "life teachers" who continue to add richness to my journey.

"To gain the most from your life journey,
treat every person you meet as a teacher
and every situation you experience as a learning opportunity."

—Eric Allenbaugh

contents

contributors

"If you want to be successful, it's just this simple: Know what you are doing, love what you are doing, and believe in what you are doing. It's just that simple."

—Will Rogers

A NUMBER OF seasoned executives and consultants have written "Deliberate Success Gems" for this book. Their carefully crafted ideas, distributed throughout book, will add value to your learning experience. I gratefully acknowledge the following "Deliberate Success Leaders" for their written contributions to this book:

- Ronald W. Allen, former Chairman, President, and CEO of Delta Air Lines, Inc.
- Colleen Barrett, President & Chief Operating Officer, Southwest Airlines
- Ken Blanchard, Ph.D., coauthor of and *Managing By Values, The One Minute Manager,* and *Leadership by the Book*

- Peter Block, Ph.D., author of *The Empowered Manager* and *Stewardship*
- James C. Collins, Ph.D., coauthor of *Built to Last*
- Dale Gifford, Chief Executive, Hewitt Associates
- Jeff Israel, M.D., Quixtar Diamond Independent Business Owner
- Michael O'Connor, Ph.D., coauthor of *The Platinum Rule* and *Managing By Values*
- Jerry I. Porras, Ph.D., coauthor of *Built to Last*
- Richard Thalheimer, Chairman, The Sharper Image
- Brian Tracy, President, Brian Tracy International
- Alex Trotman, former Chairman & CEO, Ford Motor Company
- Steve Van Andel, Chairman, Quixtar Corporation

"Never doubt that a small group of thoughtful, committed citizens can change the world; indeed, it's the only thing that ever has."

—Margaret Mead

foreword

by denis waitley, ph.D.

"Houston, we have a problem!" These infamous words came from the commander of the *Apollo 13* command module moments after it suffered an internal explosion. The resulting damage placed the three astronauts on board in extreme danger as the command module hurled through space nearly 200,000 miles from Earth.

I was in the NASA control room when those words echoed over the public-address system. I could feel the fear as silence momentarily interrupted the usual intense activity of the hundreds of scientists and engineers engaged in the Moon Mission. No one doubted the critical nature of the astronauts' circumstances: The mother ship had lost essential fuel supplies; they could not generate sufficient oxygen for the return trip to Earth; and remaining power sources were inadequate to operate the flight control instruments. In short, the *Apollo 13* mission suffered what appeared to be fatal challenges. And some of the engineers started to buy into the "impossibility" of bringing the astronauts home alive.

"Failure is not an option!" declared the *Apollo 13* Mission Control director stationed in Houston. These words both challenged and inspired the scientists and engineers to tap into their very best in dealing with a potentially catastrophic event. The Mission Control director would not accept anything but a successful outcome—even in the face of what seemed to be insurmountable odds. Efforts by others to convince him of his "unrealistic and overly optimistic" expectations of saving the three astronauts simply fell on deaf ears. The Mission Control director committed to experiencing a deliberate and successful outcome. Period!

"It's an impossible situation, but it has possibilities."

—Sam Goldwyn

What happened in the chilling hours that followed reflected the essence of my lifelong work in learning how winners prevail and how losers succumb. Some people, overwhelmed by what seemed to be overwhelming obstacles, missed the creative opportunities. Others tapped into their inner resources and drew out the very best of themselves and their team as they found ingenious solutions to problems that have never before been addressed. The losers focused on cynicism. The winners focused on synergism.

Skeptics and cynics continued to surface on the floor of the Houston Mission Control Center. Overhearing one of his superiors express grave doubts about their ability to achieve a successful outcome, the Mission Control director held firm to his convictions and boldly declared: "On the contrary, Sir, you are about to experience NASA's finest hour."

The Mission Control Director had a clear and compelling mission. He effectively engaged and empowered his team to explore and implement options in support of that mission. He held people accountable to tap into their talents and deliver their very best. He did not settle for less than success; bringing the astronauts only part way home alive did not meet his high standards!

Tapping into every available resource and pushing each person to their creative best, he listened to people at any level who had good ideas, yet ignored messages from the many skeptics who doubted his objectives and methods. In short, the Mission Control director effectively displayed the qualities of a results-oriented leader—one who commits to Deliberate Success! He modeled the power of linking purpose and passion with performance.

He and his team brought the three astronauts home alive and well. They achieved his expectations—"NASA's finest hour!" The *Apollo 13* Moon Mission provides a legendary example of deliberate efforts to create a successful outcome—and how to build a great team that delivers impressive results.

"The greatest danger for most of us
is not that our aim is too high and we miss it,
but that it is too low and we reach it."

—Michelangelo

Success is not an accident. Neither is failure. Both result from actions—or inactions—that you take in your life journey. You must learn from your past mistakes, but not lean on your past successes. You may not be responsible for the circumstances of your life, but you are responsible for the decisions you make within those circumstances. Instead of asking, "Why me?" commit to saying, "Try me!" Rather than *seeking* success, commit to a conscious, deliberate process of *bringing* success to every aspect of your personal and professional life. You must look in the mirror when you ask who is responsible for your failures and for your successes.

In reading *Deliberate Success*, you are about to embark on a mission of your own to create even more effective individual, team, and organizational results. You are your own "Mission Control Director" in your life journey and can have an even greater impact in producing the positive results you seek, both personally and professionally. Through this journey, you will be creating your own "finest hour"—time and time again.

> "Success is the progressive realization of a worthwhile goal."
>
> **—Napoleon Hill**

In *Deliberate Success*, Dr. Allenbaugh masterfully presents proven success principles and powerful implementation tools that you can immediately apply in bringing out the best of yourself, your team, and your organization. You can expect to take away from this book inspirational stories, the sage wisdom of masters in the field who contributed "Deliberate Success Gems," hundreds of pragmatic ideas, and tools you can use for a lifetime in getting from where you are to where you want to be. This book will both inspire and challenge you to be and do your best. You and other winners in life will discover the value of reading and rereading *Deliberate Success: Realizing Your Vision With Purpose, Passion, and Performance.*

—Denis Waitley, Ph.D.

Dr. Waitley's books include:
- *The Psychology of Winning*
- *Empires of the Mind: Lessons to Lead and Succeed in a Knowledge-Based World*
- *Winner's Edge: The Critical Attitude of Success*
- *Seeds of Greatness: The Ten Best-Kept Secrets of Total Success*

- *The New Dynamics of Winning: Gain the Mind-Set of a Champion For Unlimited Success in Business and Life*
- *The New Dynamics of Goal Setting: Flextactics for a Fast-Changing Future*
- *Psychology of Success: Developing Your Self-Esteem*

introduction

> "We cannot teach people anything;
> we can only help them discover it."
>
> **—Galileo**

DELIBERATE SUCCESS WILL assist you in closing the gap between where you are now and where you want to be—in business and in life. Achieving success is not an accident; it results from a deliberate process of identifying a compelling purpose, passionately pursuing your vision, preparing for high level outcomes, and performing at your best.

Most of what you are seeking "out there," however, is already inside. The answers are within. Yet I frequently hear people say, "Teach me something new!" Teach me how to create more of what I want in life. Teach me how to build an even more productive, profitable business. Many have the mistaken notion that some new, exotic idea will provide the magic answer to gain the competitive edge.

In most cases, you already "know" what you need to do, to be, to become, and to release to generate higher levels of success within your organization, within your family, and within your personal life. The art of *Deliberate Success* calls you to use what you already know at a higher level—in other words, to function with awareness and intention to create what you want in your organization and in your life.

John Wooden, the highly successful former UCLA basketball coach, led his team to more consecutive season championships than any other coach in the sport's history. Wooden, however, never focused on exotic strategies, trick plays, or gimmicks. Instead, his "success strategy" focused on doing the *fundamentals* exceptionally well. Rather than winning, he focused on mastery—doing the very best that one can. Sometimes he was toughest on the team when they won, because they did not play well. His mastery-focused, principle-centered, stick-to-the-fundamentals approach proved to be the winning formula for success over and over. And this same philosophy characterizes peak-performing companies and individuals who have long-term track records of success.

You will benefit significantly from the best practice principles and pragmatic tools explored in the **Five Success Strategies**, which are:

1. DIRECTION: Linking Purpose and Passion with Performance.
2. CULTURE: Sustaining a Results-Oriented, Customer-Focused Climate.
3. EMPOWERMENT: Releasing Human Potential.
4. COACHING: Creating Giants of Others.
5. RENEWAL: Sustaining Your Competitive Edge.

In addition to the **Five Success Strategies**, you will acquire new ways to assist individuals, teams, and your organization as a whole to move from good to great as you apply the **Three Performance Principles:**

1. Being Tough on Issues and Tender on People.
2. Honoring Differences and Aligning Talent.
3. Building the Bottom Line and the Human Element.

Each of the **3 Performance Principles** fortifies **The Power of "And."** This dual thinking links the tangible with the intangible. In peak-performing organizations, leaders are concurrently tough on issues *and* tender on people. They practice honoring differences *and* integrating those contrasting forces to serve a common direction. Finally, leaders of highly successful organizations simultaneously focus on the bottom line *and* the human element. *Deliberate Success* links the hard *and* the soft elements to create great teams that deliver impressive results. In contrast, struggling organizations make the mistaken assumption that *either* they need to generate bottom line results *or* be more relationship oriented. "Either/or" thinking contains rather than releases the best of others.

The ideas explored in *Deliberate Success* represent more than two decades of research into the principles and practices of peak-performing organizations and individuals. To provide additional value to you, I have also referenced scores of pragmatic principles and tools from master achievers with enviable track records of success. In addition to my own research and experience, "Deliberate Success Gems" from prominent leaders and consultants (their best strategies prepared especially for this book) are strategically placed throughout the chapters.

You will find yourself reaching for this success resource book time and time again as you shape your future. Count on *Deliberate Success* to provide the ideas and tools to turn purpose and passion into performance results. Applying what you learn here will assist in achieving your "finest hour"—in business and in life.

"Success is not for the ambivalent.
It's for those who know what they want and go after it,
no matter how difficult the path."

—Alex Trotman
Former Chairman & CEO, Ford Motor Company

---

deliberate success
strategy 1: direction

linking purpose and passion
with performance

"Before you can inspire with emotion,
you must be swamped with it yourself.
Before you can move their tears, your own must flow.
To convince them, you must yourself believe."

—**Winston Churchill**

chapter 1

creating a compelling mission and vision

*"If you want to build a ship,
don't drum up people together to collect wood
and don't assign them tasks and work,
but rather teach them to long for the
endless immensity of the sea."*

—Antoine de Saint-Exupery

WHEN YOU THINK of highly successful companies, what comes to mind? Dell, Nordstrom, Disney, Southwest Airlines? These and others continue to achieve outstanding results because of their compelling vision and deliberate, principle-centered actions. Clearly, success is not an accident in these companies. And success is not an accident in your life either.

Southwest Airlines has experienced more than three consecutive decades of profitability, has earned numerous awards for being the preferred airline by passengers, and is included among the very top employers to work for in all of Corporate America. By any measure of success, the company seems to have it together.

I was fortunate to be invited to one of its two-day cultural events for executives, where Southwest Airlines generously shared many of the ideas that have contributed to its long-term success. One of the nearly 150 executives present asked Colleen Barrett, President & COO, *"How do you continue to produce such positive bottom line results year after year?"* She responded, *"Two things: We follow the Golden Rule, and we are passionate about our mission."* Judging from his wrinkled forehead, the executive did not understand her response. *"Yeah,"* he inquired again, *"but how do you do this?"*

With great clarity and commitment, Colleen again responded, *"Two things: We follow the Golden Rule, and we are passionate about our mission."* Many of the visiting executives still looked confused. At that point, I said to Colleen, *"Every time you are asked a question about how Southwest Airlines does something, you respond with how you* 'be' *it."* She laughed and said, *"I never thought of it in those terms, but that's it: We* 'be' *it!"* Colleen introduced one of the most significant catalysts for success in business and in life: a commitment to "be what you seek."

Herb Kelleher, Chairman of Southwest Airlines, reinvented air travel with an approach that honors people while producing significant bottom line results. At Southwest, employees are proud to proclaim that "it's not a job, it's a crusade."[1] Imagine what could happen when you effectively link purpose, passion, and performance in your organization.

Leaders convert dreams into reality. Walt Disney said, *"If you can dream it, you can do it."* Years after Disney's death, a VIP touring Disneyland commented to his guide, *"Isn't it too bad that Walt Disney did not live to see this splendor."* The guide, as the story goes, responded: *"Disney did see it—that's why it's here!"* Deliberate Success starts with a compelling dream that engages your spirit—and the spirit of your team!

People want to believe in something of significance and want to make a contribution. Visionary leaders understand this basic human need and effectively link this individual desire with serving a larger, collective purpose. The passion and burning desire to make a difference coupled with a clear and compelling direction can move an organization from mediocrity to mastery.

Abraham Lincoln provided a clear, succinct, and timely message that united people behind a common cause. Lincoln created opportunities to convey his message in simple, reverent, and patriotic terms. Lincoln's message renewed the spirit of Americans and created a "dynamic and forceful upward spiral of action and commitment. It was far more powerful than throwing money and people at the problem. By clearly renewing his vision and then gaining acceptance and commitment, Lincoln essentially revved up, and then released, what amounted to a battalion of energy within each person."[2]

 deliberate success gem

Success Is Never Final

Contributed by
James C. Collins, Ph.D. & Jerry Porras, Ph.D.

The last thing a visionary company would ever do is follow a cookbook recipe for success, any more than Michelangelo would have bought a paint-by-numbers kit. Creating a visionary company requires huge quantities of good old-fashioned hard work; there are no short-cuts. There are no magic potions. To build a visionary company, you've got to be ready for the long, hard pull. Success is never final.

—James C. Collins, Ph.D.
and Jerry Porras, Ph.D.
Coauthors of *Built to Last*

John F. Kennedy had a vision for *"this nation to take a clearly leading role in space achievement"* when he introduced the moon mission. In a clear and stirring statement, President Kennedy proclaimed, *"We will take a man to the moon and return him to earth safely by the end of the decade. We do it, not because it is easy, but because it is hard."*

J. Willard Marriott, Jr., Chief Executive of Marriott Hotels, has sustained organizational excellence and an enviable bottom line through his strong people-development approach. Lee Iacocca transformed Chrysler Corporation with his "can do" attitude and decisive management style. Jack Welch, former Chief Executive of the General Electric Company, according to *Fortune* magazine, became the "leading master of corporate change in our time." Martin Luther King awakened the American consciousness with his visionary statement: *"I have a dream that my four little children will one day live in a nation where they will be judged not by the color of their skin, but by the content of their character."*

King and other visionary leaders did *not* declare: "I have a strategic plan!" No, they each promoted a compelling vision that touched the hearts and souls of others. They effectively engaged others in transforming the dream into reality. That's what visionary leadership is all about!

Without a clearly articulated vision, associates invent their own direction that may not necessarily serve the organization. Having neither clarity of direction nor unity of purpose results in misdirected efforts, ineffective utilization of resources, slower decision making, turf wars, greater demand for supervision, and unclear priorities.

An inspiring vision encourages excelling rather than just seeking to survive. As a catalyst for change, the vision can motivate, provide direction, and place individual efforts in a focused context.

At Scandinavian Airlines, former president Jan Carlzon linked his customer-oriented vision to "moments of truth," which he defined as any point of contact during which the customer has an opportunity to pass judgment on his business. He declared, *We don't seek to be 1,000 percent better at any one thing. We seek to be 1 percent better at one thousand things.* In only 22 months, he converted a troubled company into one of the world's best airlines with his customer service–driven vision.

"In the presence of greatness, pettiness disappears."

—Robert Fritz

Nordstrom associates are taught that "our number-one goal is to provide outstanding customer service." At Nordstrom, only one policy dominates: "Use your good judgment in all situations." "Pride in performance" drives associates at Les Schwab Tire Centers, and Hewlett Packard emphasizes "innovative people at all levels." These organizations know the value of honoring individual employee differences while aligning talent to serve a common direction.

Not just empty slogans, these powerful leadership commitments both inspire and empower associates to be and do their best. An effective vision goes far beyond slogans. A working vision becomes a fundamental corporate strategy that permeates the entire organization to convert dreams into reality. Henry Ford's vision of a car in every garage, Steve Job's vision of a computer in every home, and Mahatma Gandhi's vision of an independent India "captured the imaginations of others, mobilized resources, and reshaped the reality of their times."[3]

Visionary companies—and individuals—demonstrate a unique ability to take quantum leaps forward, manifest a significant return on investment, and even exhibit exceptional resiliency in recovering from difficult business conditions. Visionary companies such as IBM and Ford have weathered exceptionally tough times, only to move forward with greater commitment to a clearer direction.

Research by Collins and Porras in their book, *Built to Last,* demonstrates that visionary companies, over a 50-year period, produced a return of investment more than 15 times greater than that of the general market. You can take the intimate link between purpose, passion, and performance to the bank!

the navigational constellation

Vision, when combined with clarity of mission, values, and philosophy, becomes a "navigational constellation" that guides planning, decision-making, and organizational behavior. The navigational constellation guides the organization to a destination while influencing the quality of the journey. When clear about these elements, people have an internal guidance system that assists in directing their talents and energy to accomplishing a larger purpose. Leaders can capitalize on empowering others and releasing creativity rather than having to control and tightly supervise employees.

"The things that get rewarded get done."

—Michael LeBoeuf

Peter Drucker, the distinguished management consultant, encourages leaders to periodically address the following key questions:[4]

the "navigational constellation"

Mission:
What is our purpose?
Vision:
Where are we going?
Culture:
What do we value?

1. What is your mission?
2. Is it still worth doing?
3. If we were not already doing this, would we now do it?

Although the mission generally remains constant and tends to transcend time, periodically revisiting the core purpose assures that your organization remains on course. Additionally, periodic examination of the fundamental reason for being renews understanding of and commitment to the corporate direction. Mission needs to be reinforced in multiple ways and multiple times so that it creates a life of its own.

> "On course doesn't mean perfect.
> On course means that even when things don't go perfectly,
> you are still going in the right direction."
>
> **—Charles Garfield**

Walt Disney, in his hospital bed the day before he died, creatively explored the development of Disney World in Florida. This visionary instilled a corporate spirit that transcends his death. His commitment to building a company and empowering people demonstrated itself through numerous actions. In

Disney's early years, he paid his creative staff even more than himself. In the 1930s, he invested in art classes for his cartoonists, created team processes, and developed advanced animation technologies. Disney later implemented the first bonus system in his industry to attract and retain talent. Disney University has become a corporate legend in developing a strong corporate culture.[5]

Walt Disney so effectively engaged others in his vision that his dream became theirs. Although Walt Disney is but a memory, the reality of his dream continues to live on in the lives to those touched by his imagination. Disney demonstrated the power of converting his purpose and passion into reality.

What dream is developing in your own life? What legacy are you seeking to leave? How might this world be an even better place as a result of your being here? Are you following your passion? Are you "on purpose?"

---

*"Leaders are visionaries
with a poorly developed sense of fear
and no concept of the odds against them."*

**—Dr. Robert Jarvik,
inventor of the Jarvik-7, an artificial heart**

chapter 2

creating a spirit of
passion for the possible

> "Whatever you can do, or dream you can, begin in boldness.
> Boldness has genius, power, and magic in it."
>
> **—Goethe**

AT A PERSONAL growth seminar I attended a few years ago, the workshop leader had his associate brace himself with both arms outstretched and locked while holding a wood plank. The seminar leader approached with intense focus and suddenly broke through the plank with his bare hand. We marveled at his accomplishment, but soon learned that he expected us to do the same! He demonstrated how to position our hand to avoid injury and then had us each pair up with another person to take turns breaking wood planks. None of us succeeded!

Aware of our frustration, the workshop leader then introduced us to the concept of the "target behind the target." Although *our* full force and energy ended at the board, *he* just gathered momentum as he easily passed through the plank striking his imaginary target six inches beyond the board. Armed with that new information, each of us repeated our effort to break the plank. By shifting our target beyond the board, we all looked like karate masters breaking plank after plank. One woman in the session got into being macho and asked for *two* planks. Using this target behind the target concept, she easily punched through both planks simultaneously. The rest of us kept our distance from her for the rest of the seminar!

Let's apply the learning from this board-breaking exercise to life. In my experience in working with many thousands of executives and associates in hundreds of corporations, most people want to be a part of something that makes a difference. They want to contribute in some way to a larger purpose. They want to go *beyond* just producing or selling products, completing paperwork, or finishing an assignment. It's not just the "what?"—it's the "so what?" that gets people's juices flowing. That's where the "target behind the target" thinking applies. Why not think of the wood plank as the "what?" or "purpose" and the target behind the target as the "so what?" or the "purpose behind the purpose"?

Making money certainly generates interest, yet seldom taps into the passion of people. People want to be engaged with something that has greater meaning. When the larger corporate purpose goes beyond the wood plank—beyond "mere" profitability and productivity—the passion of people ignites. When leaders tap into the passion of individuals (the purpose beyond the purpose), enormous creativity and productivity can be released.

When leaders effectively link the organizational vision with the interests of associates, a catalytic action occurs. Passion, productivity, and possibility-thinking punch through barriers as people experience themselves serving a larger purpose. Paradoxically, companies practicing this philosophy generate even greater bottom-line results. Serving a larger purpose not only

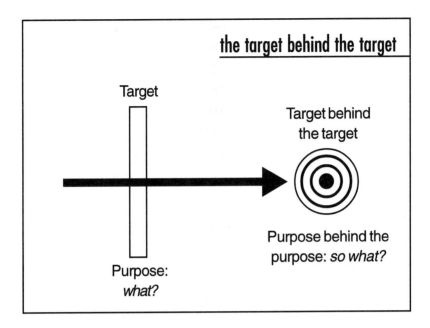

benefits our community and society, but it makes good business sense.

Roy Vagelos voiced the Merck vision in his message that "above all, let's remember that our business means victory against disease and to help mankind." Merck's altruistic drive to develop and distribute a drug to prevent river blindness in Third World countries reinforced application of its philosophy to help humankind.[6] Southwest Airlines claims that it has a "much higher calling—that of allowing people from every walk of life to see and do things they never dreamed of."[7] The "target behind the target" demonstrates that profits do not drive these organizations. Rather, profits result from pursuing the vision and practicing values that make a difference. When purpose ignites passion, performance results.

Clarity of the purpose behind the purpose engages people in their passion and promotes higher performance levels. Consider these examples:

- The *purpose* of a university is to educate; the *purpose behind the purpose* is to assist others in experiencing a more fulfilling life through education.
- The *purpose* of an insurance company is to sell policies; the *purpose behind the purpose* is to assist its clients in experiencing peace of mind.

What would you describe as the purpose of a real-estate company? Most respond with "selling houses and making money." A real-estate company retained me to assist in clarifying its purpose. Working through this process, the company modified its mission to "assisting families to find and move into their dream home." By shifting focus from meeting its own needs to serving the interests of its clients, the company's profits soared as a result of the many internal changes made to fulfill the new mission and to delight its clients.

When leaders and staff integrate the "purpose behind the purpose" into their way of being and doing, things begin to happen. People look for ways of serving what they now understand to be a higher purpose. The more challenging and inspiring the purpose, the more likely people are to function at their best.

guidelines for developing "passion for the possible"

The following example of a hospital mission statement demonstrates the principles of integrating the target and the target behind the target. It speaks to the "what?" and the "so what?" factors essential to engage the passion of people while serving a common purpose. To build understanding of and commitment to the strategic direction, key stakeholders actively participated in its development, including the board, physicians, leadership, and staff. Knowing that people support that which they help to create, the highly participatory process resulted in the following "navigational constellation."

medical center strategic direction

Our mission: (What is our purpose?)

Our commitment is to enhance the quality of lives of those we touch (the target behind the target) through providing comprehensive, integrated, and accessible health care services (the target).

Our vision: (Where are we going?)

As a center for wellness and healing, our vision is to:

- Make a significant and positive contribution to both individual and public health in our service area.
- Become recognized as the regional center of healthcare excellence in both treatment and prevention.
- Become the premier managed-care provider in this region through prudent positioning of our inpatient, outpatient, and health education services.

Our culture: (What do we value?)

We commit to creating a distinctive culture that:

- Honors patients, families, staff, physicians, and all those with whom we interact.
- Responds with personal commitment, human sensitivity, and technical excellence.
- Creates a healing environment that models the following core values in everything we do:
  - Respect.
    - Integrity.
      - Service.
        - Excellence.

★★★

A lofty goal? Certainly! As Stephen Covey says, *"Everything is created twice—first in your mind and then in reality."* Leaders first have a dream, then they convert that dream into tangible results. Leaders energize the vision with an intangible spirit and tangible actions. An idealistic vision statement conveys hope and stimulates people to stretch to new levels of performance and commitment. The second creation (in reality) cannot happen without the first creation (the dream).

When a critical mass of people intends to accomplish a clearly defined outcome, things begin to happen. In fact, every major change in the world has started with an individual or small group who felt passionately about accomplishing something important. A bold mission and vision get people's creative juices flowing and stimulate courage in addressing the tough issues. People replace negative thinking with possibility thinking. The possible begins to take form. The "impossible" takes just a little longer.

Before meaningful progress can be made, you need to clearly define where you want to be. Your strategic direction has a major impact in directing talent and resources toward a desired result while creating a distinctive competitive position. IBM's mission, for example, has focused on being a service-oriented computer company, whereas Apple's focus is on being user-friendly. The Oregon Department of Education accepts the challenge to be "in the relentless pursuit of each student's success." Notice how the mission can be a compelling call to action. The Mission Effectiveness Profile on the facing page will assist in assessing the value of your own strategic direction statement.

In the mastery organization, mission, vision, and values become the driving forces behind planning, decision-making, problem-solving, and day-to-day operations. These become a

mission effectiveness profile

success criteria	your success rating low high
1. To what extent is the core purpose broad enough to be inclusive, yet narrow enough to provide clear enough direction in aligning all parts of the organization?	1 2 3 4 5
2. To what extent does the mission clearly identify the organization's purpose (your business) and the purpose behind the purpose (the passion)?	1 2 3 4 5
3. To what extent is the mission easy to communicate to key stakeholders?	1 2 3 4 5
4. To what extent does the mission link organizational with individual interests and ignite their spirit?	1 2 3 4 5
5. To what extent does the mission demonstrate value to your clients or customers, a difference they would be willing to select you over your competitors?	1 2 3 4 5
6. To what extent can leaders and associates effectively implement the mission in producing meaningful results?	1 2 3 4 5
7. To what extent have the benefits of carrying out the strategic direction been fully identified and effectively communicated to the various stakeholders?	1 2 3 4 5
8. To what extent have the risks or costs of *both* carrying out the mission and *not* carrying out the mission been fully explored?	1 2 3 4 5
9. To what extent does the mission distinguish you from your competitors?	1 2 3 4 5
10. To what extent are board members, the CEO, the leadership team, and associates committed to doing whatever it takes to convert the mission into tangible results?	1 2 3 4 5

way of life, not just words on a piece of paper. When you integrate mission and vision with who you are and what you do, you both shape and manifest your destiny.

vision keepers: the 7th-generation principle

"A man has made at least a start on discovering the meaning of human life when he plants shade trees under which he knows he will never sit."

Elton Trueblood

Leaders of the Iroquois Confederacy historically gathered their "wisdom-keepers" to address significant issues of concern to their Indian nation. The wise men challenged themselves to evaluate significant plans and issues in the context of honoring the spirit of the Iroquois mission and vision and meeting both *present* and *future* generation needs. Although I am taking some literary license with their concept, they essentially asked this: How will this decision affect our people seven generations from now? And what will our people, seven generations from now, be thanking us for having had the courage to address, and what might they be cursing us for failing to deal with effectively? These are important questions for leaders—even today.

At a hospital board strategic-planning retreat I facilitated, the board members expressed grave concern about the future of their landlocked and increasingly obsolete facility. Significant expansion of their current hospital could not be accomplished at the existing location. Population-growth trends demonstrated movement away from the hospital's existing location. Although the need to move to a new site seemed relatively obvious, a significant dilemma immediately confronted them: A number of physician office buildings surrounded the hospital, and those physicians strongly opposed moving the hospital to a new location. The physicians had a strong financial interest in staying at the current site. What to do?

I introduced to the board members the 7th-Generation Principle of the Iroquois Confederacy: "Imagine even 20 years from now that your successors are in this room looking back to the decision you are about to make today. Twenty years from now, what will that future board be thanking you for having had the courage to address and what might they be cursing you for failing to deal with effectively?"

Met at first with reflective silence, the 7th-Generation Principle stimulated their collective thought process. Ideas then started gushing as if creative floodgates had opened. The next generation of board members would of course expect a decision to move to a new location. To do anything else would jeopardize the hospital's future and contribute to its demise.

In spite of strong pressure to meet current needs at the expense of the long-term future, the board decided to purchase land at a location that would effectively serve future generations. They also began the process of creatively exploring win-win options for the relocation of physicians who had invested in office buildings at the current site. The board exercised courage in making a principled decision that made a positive, long-term difference. They honored the spirit of the 7th-Generation Principle.

Leaders have a simultaneous responsibility to pay attention to short- and long-term implications of their decisions. Too often, short-term operational needs take precedence over long-term interests. Managers are often pressured to make decisions that make the quarterly financial reports look good while simultaneously creating long-term problems. They mistakenly conclude that either today's *or* tomorrow's needs will be met—but not both. This limited either-or thinking creates a short-term "solution" that inevitably becomes a long-term problem.

Keeping the vision alive remains one of the most important challenges of leadership. Leaders who make a difference dream bold dreams, have the courage to walk their talk, and martial the resources necessary to manifest the vision in meeting present and future interests. Leaders become the corporate "vision-keepers" through every action.

Are you "voicing your vision?" Are you clear about your purpose and your purpose behind the purpose? Are you engaging others in both the short-term needs and long-term interests? Are you turning purpose and passion into performance results?

"Passion is something that starts in the gut,
floods the imagination, and comes to reside in the will.
Passion is disciplined when it has focus,
consistency, persistence, and, above all, integrity."

—James Kouzer and Berry Posner

chapter 3

implimenting your vision:

strategies for success

*"At the very beginning, I had a very clear picture
of what the company would look like
when it was finally done...
I realized that for IBM to become a great company
it would have to act like a great company
long before it ever became one."*

—Tom Watson, Founder of IBM

HOW DO YOU get from where you are now to where you want to be? *"Begin with the end in mind,"* encourages Stephen Covey. Then, realize your vision with each moment-to-moment decision that you make. By first clarifying your big-picture outcome, creativity can be released and directed to achieving the corporate vision. The visionary end-state becomes an internal guide, giving purpose and clarity to each action you take in achieving your vision.

Implementation strategies must be developed and account-abilities assigned. Tracking systems follow progress on each of the major themes; milestones are monitored, successes are celebrated, and corrective action is taken to assure that the organization produces consistently with the strategic direction.

Members of your team can be great resources in addressing how you get from where you are to where you want to be. When engaged in a safe process of co-creating the desired state, team members build understanding of the purpose, develop that important sense of passion, and ultimately focus their talent on service to the vision. Engage your team in such important questions as:

- What is your understanding of the direction we are going?
- What are some of the more critical internal and external reasons for pursuing that direction?
- What do you see as the benefits and possible pitfalls of that direction?
- What consequences might we experience if we do not pursue that direction?
- How can we build greater support from such key stakeholders as employees, unions, management, suppliers, and customers?
- What future talent will be required to support that vision?
- How can we go about preparing and training people most effectively to successfully achieve those big picture results?
- To load the process for Deliberate Success, what business practices and systems do we need to change and how can we change them to effectively support the new vision?

Exploring these questions with your team and key stakeholders in advance of the changes will build support and facilitate

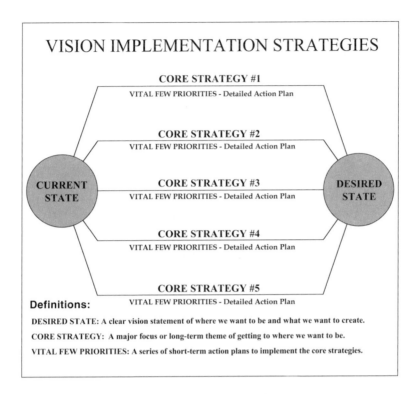

delivery of impressive results. Load your process for success by doing your homework and advance team building.

Consider the strategic model of getting from where you are to where you want to be, as seen above. Working backwards from your vision, enlist key stakeholders in developing an action plan consisting of "core strategies" and related "vital few priorities."

"No problem can stand the assault of sustained thinking."

Voltaire

Core strategies become driving forces within the organization to achieve results in alignment with the strategic direction.

Each of your recommended five to eight core-strategy statements should start with an action word, be positively stated, and generate a sense of fervor. A healthcare client, for example, developed a corporate vision of creating a comprehensive, integrated healthcare system in its service area. Its core strategies included:

- Create and maintain a healing environment of benefit to both patients and staff.
- Build a spirit of partnership with physicians, employees, and third-party payers.
- Create a responsive, customer-focused organization that functions with quality and sensitivity.
- Expand our market share to 60% within five years.
- Maintain our fiscal viability while developing a competitive cost advantage.
- Simplify systems and organizational structure to assure effective, efficient operations.

To assure timely achievement of results, a "corporate sponsor" was assigned to each core strategy. Although not necessarily responsible for doing the actual work, the corporate sponsor serves as a vision-keeper, a facilitator, and a point person for his or her respective core strategy. These people actively market and promote the core strategy; assemble talented, committed people to develop specific action plans; and serve as bureaucracy busters in punching through organizational red tape.

The core strategies became a unifying force that integrated various elements of the growing organization while providing a framework for individual departments and divisions to develop their own goals consistent with the overall vision. The entire organization began to more effectively synthesize its collective efforts to sustain peak performance consistent with a shared purpose and vision.

deliverables: putting your priorities into action

Building accountability for "deliverables" (specific short-term outcomes) can enhance attaining and sustaining performance results consistent with the mission and vision. Each individual, team, and department should have clear "vital few priorities" that specifically address measurable outcomes, each of which brings the organization closer to realization of your big picture goals. Challenge yourself and others to do the right thing. Only actions that bring you closer to realization of the mission and vision should be awarded key resources—time, talent, and treasure.

Within each core strategy, establish "vital few priorities" to provide tangible action steps scheduled for accomplishment within the next year. This is where the rubber hits the road. Moving from the general to the specific, action teams develop specific, measurable tactical objectives that support the mission, vision, and core strategies.

Core strategies typically guide the organizational direction over a several-year period; vital few priorities address here-and-now issues calling for attention. Action plans ultimately identify *who* does *what* by *when*. This degree of specificity with identified accountabilities and measurable outcomes places creative stress to perform consistently with the corporate direction.

At least once a quarter, I encourage leaders and staff to assemble to reinforce mission and vision, assess progress on each of the core strategies, monitor tangible progress regarding each of the vital few priorities, celebrate successes, and take corrective action. The process itself provides creative stress for individuals to convert their "deliverables" into tangible results. When peers gather in the strategic planning room to assess results, no one wants to come into that meeting without demonstrating positive results regarding his assignments. This systematic process of moving from the long-term mission to short-term deliverables builds understanding of and alignment with the corporate strategic direction.

Celebrating successes—even the little ones—builds passion for performance and encourages people to continue to do their best. When deliverables are not achieved, have the courage to take corrective action and respectfully hold people accountable by looking for the learning and self-correcting.

Development of a compelling vision does not guarantee results. You must commit yourself and organizational resources to converting the vision into measurable deliverables. Goals, strategies, systems, roles, and day-to-day tactics must reflect the vision. Look for opportunities to reinforce the vision, encourage others, celebrate successes, and self-correct.

Examine your role as a vision-keeper. Are you challenging yourself and others to reflect the vision in every aspect of your work? Are your decisions and actions bringing your vision closer to reality? Are you delivering results that count? Are you shaping your organizational culture to be "on purpose?"

"A vision is only an idea or an image
of a more desirable future for the organization,
but the right vision is an idea so energizing
that it in effect jump-starts the future
by calling forth the skills, talents,
and resources to make it happen."

—Burt Nanus

---

deliberate success
strategy 2: culture

sustaining a results-oriented, customer-focused climate

"Anyone who says they work
just for the money
has given up the hope
that anything more
is possible."

—Peter Block

chapter 4

corporate culture:

the invisible driving force

"Not everything that counts can be counted."

—Denis Burkitt

CORPORATE CULTURE IS that invisible driving force that reflects the collective values and behavior of those associated with the organization. It determines what is accomplished, who gets hired and promoted, and how decisions are made. It conditions what gets communicated, what is important, how people dress, and how employees feel about the organization. Culture influences the way employees act, how customers respond, and ultimately what The Bottom Line looks like.

Declaration of vision and values from top management does not necessarily produce a culture. Culture slowly emerges from accumulation of the moment-by-moment, decision-by-decision, and action-by-action activities that reflect what leaders pay attention to in the organization. Clearly, actions speak louder than words in forming the corporate culture.

Because culture has such a profound impact on productivity, morale, and customer service, shaping corporate culture becomes a core strategy of enlightened leaders. They do not leave formation of culture to chance. Instead, leaders consciously and deliberately seek to positively influence that invisible driving force to turn purpose and passion into productive results. Leaders who do not vigorously shape the culture will ultimately find themselves being shaped by the culture itself.

Southwest Airlines demonstrates a vigorous commitment to developing and nurturing a strong culture, starting with "hiring for attitude and training for skill." Colleen Barrett, President & COO of Southwest, prepared the following that captures the essence of a peak performing culture.

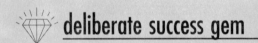 **deliberate success gem**

The Southwest Airlines "Warrior Spirit"

Contributed by Colleen Barrett

The culture of Southwest Airlines is characterized by a positive, can-do, intense spirit—a "Warrior Spirit." We don't do anything partway. We function at our very best when challenged. That's the way it's been from the very beginning. And it continues to shape who we are.

Even before we put our first airplane in the sky, we litigated for three and one-half years. The "big guys" in the airline industry challenged our right to fly and challenged our every move. They wanted to keep us grounded. But we had—and continue to have—a mission.

Herb Kelleher, our then-founder and now chairman, knew nothing about running an airline. But he knew a lot about justice, fair play, mission, and spirit. Every roadblock the big guys threw up seemed to stir, then incite, a basic survival instinct within each of us in the early days. That awakening spirit became contagious and started to settle in with our troops.

Instead of feeling depressed and defeated, our small group of employees developed a fire in their bellies. The Southwest Airlines "Warrior Spirit" was born. On their own time, 200 employees distributed flyers on the street corners, supported Herb in court, and took the initiative to develop their guerilla fighting skills at every opportunity. They had a mission. They were determined to win. And nothing would stop them.

The "Warrior Spirit" developed out of necessity. We didn't plan it; it was not someone's great leadership idea. It simply evolved from difficult circumstances. But we soon became aware of how important the "Warrior Spirit" is to our mission, our culture, and our way of being. Incredible pride developed from our early accomplishments, and people learned how much they can achieve when they put their heart and soul into something that makes a positive difference. Early on, passion for our mission, following The Golden Rule, and "doing the right thing" shaped the culture of Southwest Airlines. Paying attention to these basic beliefs continues to be our way. Although we are far from perfect and continue to make mistakes, we are learning and growing together.

"Always do the right thing. That will gratify some of the people and astonish the rest."

—Mark Twain

Keeping the "Warrior Spirit" alive and kicking at Southwest Airlines is now a major leadership and cultural priority. We encourage and nurture the "Warrior Spirit." With pride, we internally share story after story about how our employees confront challenges, overcome obstacles, provide positively outrageous service for customers, and "do the right thing." We consider every employee to be a leader, and we expect all employees to give their best. Funny thing—they seem to consistently rise to that level of expectation.

The "Warrior Spirit" shows up in many ways and continues to both distinguish us from other airlines and to be a source of pride. We fight during the hard times and celebrate during the good times. Let me share a couple examples:

- During the Gulf War, fuel prices skyrocketed and challenged our fiscal viability. Confronted with the same problem, other airlines were already operating in the red and having to cut back. A Southwest cargo-department employee, on his own, took action to protect our company during this difficult time. He put the word out among the other employees that the company had always been there for them, and now it was the employees' turn to be there for the company. He started a "Fuel From The Heart" movement, resulting in a large number of Southwest Employees voluntarily taking a payroll deduction to help pay for the rising fuel costs. We stayed in the black and did not lay off any employees.

- When Midway Airlines pulled out of Chicago, we immediately flew a team of 20 Southwest employees to set up shop. By the next day (the next day!), Southwest Airlines had scheduled service out of our newly renovated gates—less than 24 hours after our competitor pulled out. We moved so quickly that the news media did not even have time to film us putting our signs up at the new gates. The television crews asked us to take our signs down and put then them back up, just so they could "catch us in the act" of starting service from there. We were too fast. We do everything in record time. We have to be nimble like a cat. Were these new Midway gates in our master plan? No. We don't even have a master plan! We operate from our mission. Did we form a committee to conduct a feasibility study before acting? No. We just did the right thing. We don't want employees bound by a bunch of rules—we want them to use their best judgment.

Guided by our mission and fueled by our passion, we don't back away from challenges; we welcome them. We get concerned, however, when we get so much publicity about our successes. Success is never final. Victory is never final. Every time we reach a higher level of performance, new challenges, new customer expectations, and new technology give us a swift kick in the rear. We will always have to tap into our "Warrior Spirit" to make a great company even greater.

—Colleen Barrett
President & Chief Operating Officer,
Southwest Airlines
www.southwestair.com

Southwest does not leave development of the culture up to chance. Every operational location has its "Culture Committee" actively engaged in keeping the "Warrior Spirit" alive. The leaders of Southwest Airlines (every employee is considered to be a leader) carefully orchestrate and nurture their culture to create a spirit of partnership in everything they do. They look out for each other and they pull together when the going gets tough. And it pays off.

The tragic terrorist attacks of September 11, 2001, had a particularly traumatic impact on the airline industry. Almost all U.S. domestic airlines experienced major financial losses and were compelled to lay off thousands of employees—except one airline. The "Warrior Spirit" of Southwest's employees kicked in with fierce loyalty and determination to keep the planes flying and to keep employees on the payroll. Many donated unpaid hours of work, some turned their tax surplus rebates over to the company, and others volunteered to take over lawncare at the corporate headquarters. They pulled together once again to save enough money to keep their 30,000-member family intact. According to CNN just a month after the attacks, "Southwest Airlines managed to post a third-quarter profit Thursday despite the September 11th terrorist attack, the only major airline that will end the period in the black." Does culture count? I think so!

the 4 corporate cultures

Just as every individual has a unique personality, every organization has a unique culture. Similar to personality differences, some aspects of the culture can be helpful and productive while other elements can detract from overall effectiveness.

In creating and sustaining Deliberate Success, leaders need to clarify the organizational targets, build on existing strengths, and work through opportunities for improvement. Aware, sensitive leaders address these critical actions in context of their unique culture. Some organizational cultures, for example, welcome this commitment to growth and development; other cultures vigorously resist change and focus on obstacles.

In my consulting work with many hundreds of organizations, I have noted that four major cultural themes tend to dominate

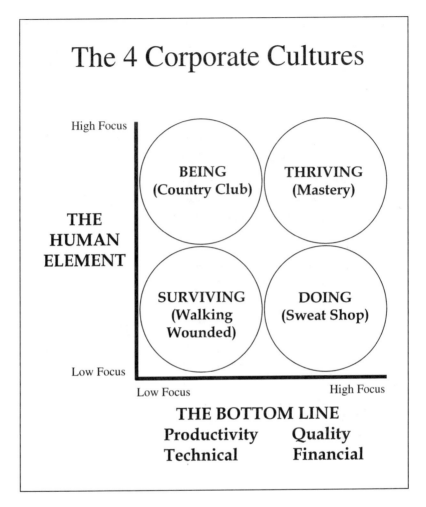

The 4 Corporate Cultures

High Focus

THE
HUMAN
ELEMENT

BEING
(Country Club)

THRIVING
(Mastery)

SURVIVING
(Walking
Wounded)

DOING
(Sweat Shop)

Low Focus

Low Focus   High Focus

THE BOTTOM LINE
Productivity   Quality
Technical   Financial

Corporate America:

1. Surviving.
2. Doing.
3. Being.
4. Thriving.

These themes result from how organizations integrate the relationship between The Human Element *and* The Bottom Line. (The origin of this principle can be traced back to the ancient

Chinese concept of *yin* [The Human Element] and *yang* [The Bottom Line] and further developed by Blake and Mouton.[8] Many of these "old truths" continue to find their way into "cutting-edge" leadership principles we practice.)

"Of all the beautiful truths pertaining to the soul
which have been restored and brought to light in this age,
none is more gladdening or fruitful of divine promise and confidence than this—
that you are the master of your thought, the molder of your character,
and the maker and shaper of condition, environment, and destiny."

—James Allen

Because the **4 Corporate Cultures** reflect the relationship between The Bottom Line *and* The Human Element, let's first take a closer look at these two dimensions. The Bottom Line focuses on the tangible, measurable elements: productivity, quality, technical, and financial. How well is your organization performing on the following key success factors?

1. **Productivity**: To what extent are you consistently producing the quantity of goods and services you are organized to produce?
2. **Quality**: To what extent are you producing those goods and services with world-class quality—quality that keeps customers coming back for more?
3. **Technology**: To what extent do your technology and systems support world-class results?
4. **Fiscal Viability**: To what extent have you positioned your organization for short and long-term fiscal viability?

The second key measure, The Human Element, represents those intangible success factors that play a significant role in achieving results. For those corporate cultures at the *lower* end of The Human Element continuum, the organizational behavior will likely result in:

- Poor communications and numerous "parking lot" meetings.
- Turf issues, "we/they" stuff, and low trust levels.
- Low morale and disengaged employees.
- A large TGIF ("Thank God it's Friday) contingency.

At the *upper* end of The Human Element scale, the culture will likely reflect:

- A strong level of teamwork and partnership.
- Caring, respectful, and open communication.
- Actively engaged, positive, productive employees.
- A TGIM ("Thank God it's Monday) contingency of employees who look forward to coming to work!

Each of the **4 Corporate Cultures** can be defined in terms of how they relate to The Bottom Line and The Human Element. Which cultural category does your organization fit in, and what are the long-term implications?

the "doing" ("sweatshop") culture: tough on issues and tough on people

The "Doing" culture focuses on achieving high productivity and profitability at the expense of the people. This pressure-cooker culture uses up people and creates a "sweatshop" environment. Management sucks talent out of the employees and rewards accomplishments with more work! Seldom are people acknowledged or appreciated. When someone does something particularly well, a typical management response is, *"That's why I pay him the big bucks!"* On the other hand, when someone makes a mistake, it's announced on a broadcast e-mail for all to see. In this culture, no news is good news.

In the "Doing" culture, taking risks can be risky business. One client president, while pointing a finger to his executive team, warned, *"I want you people to take risks—and you better not make any mistakes!"* And he was serious! What do you suppose happened to risk-taking in that organization? What about creativity? Employees found it unsafe to bring up controversial issues. Managers found it unsafe to question parts of the strategic direction that needed to be challenged. Everyone found it unsafe to explore creative options. Rather than bringing out the creative best in people, "group-think" became a way of life. Like ducks in a row, they all got in line behind their "leader." They traded off their talents, creativity, and spirit to become obedient followers. Read on how this president's perpetuation of a task-oriented culture created costly results:

> *The president's corner office overlooked the executive parking lot. Each of the executive team members had his or her name identified on their own parking space—and not for status purposes. The president used the parking stalls for role taking! He worked unusually long hours and expected his associates to do the same. By just glancing out his window either early in the morning or late at night, he could measure their level of "dedication" to the job.*
>
> *In a session I had with just the vice presidents, one confided to the group that he sometimes drove his car to work and took a taxi home! Upon hearing this, another vice president asked, "You do that too?" People play amazing games just to keep their sanity and life balance in a dysfunctional organization.*

Not surprisingly, each of the vice presidents had his or her resume polished up and was actively seeking other employment opportunities. Even the chief operating officer, the person who brought me into the organization, telephoned me one Sunday afternoon and said, "Eric, I have got to get out of here. Two more vice presidents resigned this week."

The president's command and control style did generate impressive bottom-line results—for a while. Because of using up people, however, he could not sustain high levels of performance. His board finally took action and gave him a career opportunity elsewhere!

In the long run, the sweatshop culture generally cannot sustain high levels of performance. They are into "Doing" and miss the "Being." Human resources are negated rather than nurtured. Machines, facilities, and financial systems are given more care and attention than their human counterparts. High turnover, grievances, industrial accidents, and employee unrest all contribute to an increasing cost of doing business. These same factors eventually have a negative impact on productivity. Although this strategy can work in the short to medium range, the long-term success of the company remains at serious risk.

In this environment, managers tend to focus on the visible or tangible elements of running a business. They understand and relate to the concrete nature of profits, productivity, financial ratios, quantitative analysis, and quality variations—all-important factors that certainly require attention. Their comfort with these visible indicators, however, is equally matched by their discomfort with the invisible qualities of leading an organization. The Sweatshop leaders struggle with the invisible factors: empowerment, passion, synergy, teamwork, feedback, loyalty, ownership, trust, acknowledgement, celebrations, and humor. Although they often pay lip service to these invisible factors, the importance assigned pales by comparison to the time and attention directed to the more tangible elements.

Managers in the "Doing" culture fail to comprehend the long-term value of how the invisible elements contribute to the bottom line. They miss the point that employees, especially those driven by a purpose, ultimately outperform those driven by fear. Bosses who focus on The Bottom Line without nurturing The Human Element eventually lose their competitive edge to their more aware competitors.

"Everything that you are against weakens you; everything that you are for empowers you."

—Wayne Dyer

the "being" ("country club") culture: tender on people and tender on issues

"Tender on people and tender on the issues" characterizes the culture of this organization. It focuses on The Human Element and misses The Bottom Line. The primary focus is on relationships! People are sensitive to one another and spend a great deal of time processing feelings.

At first glance, one might conclude that the Country Club organization would be a highly fulfilling culture in which to work. But dissatisfaction eventually creeps into the corporate environment. Why? People feel a need to contribute, to accomplish something worthwhile, and to make a difference. In this organizational culture, relationships take a higher priority than productivity. The Bottom Line seems to get lost through all the relating and processing. People simply do not accomplish anything worthwhile. Both the organization and the individuals suffer in the long-run.

One "Country Club" organization I am familiar with involved five social workers that formed a group practice. They had an altruistic philosophy of providing quality services to their clients, even if the clients could not afford to pay. As partners in their new company, each contributed her life savings to fund the business start-up.

Their new business developed briskly as clients took advantage of their quality services. Many clients, however, failed to pay. Within a few months, this human-oriented company experienced a fatal blow to The Bottom Line. The firm soon went out of business, and each owner lost her entire life savings.

A savvy sister administrator of a Catholic hospital once said, *"No margin, no mercy!"* She understood the need for bottom-line results. Being caring and sensitive to The Human Element at the expense of The Bottom Line may work in the short run, yet ignores the tangible factors of profits and productivity that must be maintained for long-term viability. In my more than two decades of consulting work, I have never worked with a "Country Club" organization. They are not in business long enough!

"Drive the business or it will drive thee."

—Benjamin Franklin

---

the "surviving" ("walking wounded") culture: majoring in minors and resisting risk-taking

Organizations (and individuals) in survival mode have no focus other than risk avoidance. They address neither The Bottom Line nor The Human Element. Managers in this type of organization are paralyzed by fear—fear of failure or fear of success. They lack direction, mission, and vision. They lack passion. They lack vitality. And they lack having a future!

Instead of using their creative energies to address the many issues requiring attention, representatives of this culture tend to "circle the wagons" to protect themselves from changing internal and external forces. They avoid dealing with the tough issues related to both The Human Element and The Bottom Line. They are masters at creating rules and inventing bureaucratic "solutions." Walking Wounded cultures convert energy into solid waste.

Important issues are often ignored in favor of dealing with more trivial procedural or process issues. Walking Wounded cultures micromanage until the entire business succumbs to inertia. They major in minors and ignore important issues. People feel de-energized and disempowered. By the end of their workday, emotional constipation takes its toll—it's like trying to swim in peanut butter.

When working with a group of first-line supervisors from a "Surviving" organization, I asked a number of diagnostic questions, including, *"What do you like about work?"* They responded, *"Weekends and vacations!"* Can you imagine working in this type of organization? The following account provides a shining example of a "Surviving" culture:

> *A new CEO invited me to work with the "Surviving" organization he recently inherited. He needed external consulting resources to address some very tough issues in changing the culture. We had our work cut out for us, for bureaucracy and risk avoidance characterized this organization's way of being.*
>
> *Even before showing up at the site, I received a 20-page contract related to the initial four days of planned consulting services. A team of attorneys from its contract-*

compliance department created this weighty document in an effort to assure that the organization would experience absolutely no risk during the organization development process.

The contract compliance department also sent to me a starter kit of affirmative-actions forms. I was to complete one per month for the rest of time to assure that my company had a compliant affirmative-action plan. At the time, my solo practice consulting firm had only one employee: me. Initiating an affirmative action program for my company made no sense under the circumstances.

I discarded all but one of the affirmative-action forms. I completed that single form and mailed it in with an attached note stating that this is the only form they can expect to receive from me. I also checked "Hispanic" in the racial category because of my mother's Mexican heritage. I could almost hear their elation upon learning that my consulting firm was 100-percent minority-owned and -operated! Give me a break.

It didn't end there. I received a call from one of the contract compliance attorneys requesting that I change my automobile insurance to name their organization as an insured. I asked why that was necessary. The attorney responded, "If while driving and thinking about us you are involved in an accident, we will be covered!" I didn't change my insurance.

In spite of the ingrained bureaucracy and lethargic thinking, the new, visionary CEO had the courage and tenacity to create a compelling new direction, to fire up the spirit, and to make the tough decisions. And that's when things began to happen.

Majoring in minors and avoiding risk-taking seems to be the primary focus of the "Surviving" organization. Although these organizations are quite busy dealing with their self-imposed bureaucracy, they accomplish relatively little of significance. These organizations epitomize the idea of rearranging the deck chairs on the *Titanic* as the ship sinks.

"If nothing changes, nothing changes."

—Earnie Larsen

---

the "thriving" ("mastery") culture: tough on issues and tender on people

The "Thriving" organizational culture has a vastly different orientation from any of the previously described cultures. In these Mastery or peak-performing organizations, a *dual focus* permeates the way of thinking and acting. Both leaders and staff consciously commit to creating excellence on both The Bottom Line *and* The Human Element. They shape their corporate culture by bringing out the best of "doing-ness" and "being-ness." In this organization, leaders and associates work together in a spirit of partnership to produce positive results while building a fulfilling work environment.

Does this sound like utopia? Although Mastery is but a distant dream to some managers, I have worked with a number of both private and public sector organizations that fit the Mastery criteria. The leadership and staff in these organizations are no different from you; they just apply the principles. Deliberate Success is but a decision away for most organizations.

I don't mean to oversimplify, yet the "no-magic magic" of these "Thriving" organizations results from leaders who, at each decision point, act in a way that is principle-centered *and* value-driven. They address The Bottom Line *and* The Human Element simultaneously. They come from an inner place of balance between both "doing-ness" *and* "being-ness." They consciously practice "The Power of *And!*"

The old fable about the goose that laid the golden eggs reinforces the same concept. In the "Doing" culture, the goose is killed to get the last golden egg. The "Being" environment names the goose, pets the goose, and feeds it gourmet goose food. No eggs! The "Surviving" culture asks, "What goose? What eggs?" The "Thriving" culture, however, honors and takes care of the goose while receiving a plentiful and ongoing supply of golden eggs.

In the "Thriving" organization, people experience a certain degree of ease as they move to great heights of performance. In this "Mastery" culture, people do an amazing thing: They talk to each other! Face-to-face connections take priority over memos and e-mails. Communications are simple, direct, and authentic. There's no second-guessing as to what the real message is about. People actively seek to be on each other's team and work in the spirit of partnership. They see the big picture and celebrate even minor successes in moving closer to what they want to create. People are released and empowered to effectively use their talents while edging the organization closer to realization of its overall mission and vision.

One of my clients, performing at the "Mastery" level, accomplished a major five-year goal in only four months! Another completed a five- to seven-year goal in only 11 months. And another fulfilled an 18-month goal in less than five months. How can this be? At each choice point, team members in the "Mastery" organization reinforce their strategic direction and honor their values. They pay attention to the basics and do the basics exceptionally well. When purpose and passion is turned into performance, exceptional results occur.

When you assess your own organization, which of the **4 Corporate Cultures** does your organization fit in and what are the implications? How does your culture impact the people, their commitment, and their productivity? Examine who you hire, who you promote, what you measure, what you reward, and the importance of customer service. Your responses to those questions reveal much about what your culture really values. And what you value ultimately shapes your future.

"The hard stuff is easy. The soft stuff is hard."

—Tom Peters

chapter 5

creating a
value-driven culture

WHILE WAITING IN the lobby to see the president of a light industrial business, I observed the company mission and value statement prominently displayed in an attractive frame on the wall. Its professed commitment to "customer service, quality, respect, and integrity" sounded inviting and comforting. I wondered, however, if this prospective client was serious about those important messages.

It didn't take long to experience a significant gap between what the company said and what it practiced. After inviting me into his office, the president barked several orders to his associates, then proceeded to describe how incompetent employees had created financial losses. He proclaimed that it had been necessary to sue several former employees, to sue a few key customers for breach of contract, and to sue suppliers for failure to perform. In meeting with his associates, I learned that profits were king, and that anything was justified to make a dollar. Each of the employees talked about how some products were altered to favor the company at the expense of the customer. I found myself retreating from this consulting relationship. The company continues to struggle and perhaps will until the inevitable "going out of business" auction.

Corporate values—jargon, rhetoric, or reality? A value is only a theory until it is put into practice. Executives in "Mastery" organizations commit to clarifying their corporate values and consciously applying their values — especially when the going gets tough. What you say matters. What you do matters even more. Leading by values shapes the organizational culture, defines who you are, and creates the results you experience. But leading by values requires an ongoing commitment by both leaders and associates.

Stephen Covey draws upon a poignant example of how trustworthiness is a function of character and competence:

> *If you had an honest doctor who was not competent, then you would not want him to do your surgery. If you had a competent surgeon who lacked integrity, you would not be sure if the surgery should even be done. Character comes out of personal development, competence comes out of professional development.*

Character and competence, although fundamental to individual achievement and prosperity, provide a strong and critical base for long-term business success.

"Know your truth, speak your truth, live your truth."

Eileen Hannegan

---

putting your content into context

Alignment of actions with values becomes the heart and soul of building a principle-centered business. When values are congruent with planning, problem-solving, policy formation, priority-setting, and customer service, people can perform at their best. Acting within that context provides clarity of direction and unity of purpose. Principle-centered, value-based leadership builds a positive corporate culture that produces on The Bottom Line while creating an environment of trust and partnership.

Values are those deep-seated beliefs that provide you with a code of conduct that governs both your attitudes and behavior. To learn more about what you personally value, you need to look no further than your checkbook and your calendar. And it's not much different in organizations. Financial and time priorities say a great deal about organizational values.

To make a difference, leaders need to convert values from a mere concept into tangible actions in every element of the organization. Each decision provides a choice point in which leaders and team members are encouraged to align values with actions by addressing these two critical questions:

1. Is what I am doing right now bringing us closer to where we want to be?
2. Is what I am doing right now honoring the spirit of the values we say are important?

"Decisions are easy when values are clear."

—Roy Disney

It is not the circumstances that determine who you are; it is your response to those circumstances that speaks volumes about

Walking Your Talk!

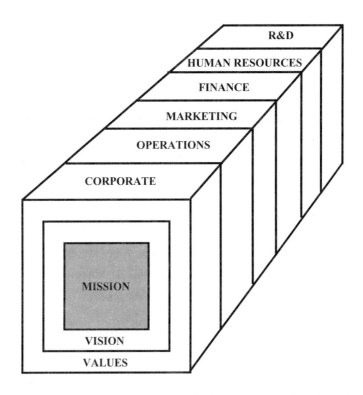

what you really value. Making principle-centered, value-driven decisions—in other words, "walking your talk"—characterizes peak-performing individuals and organizations.

It's easy to talk principled decision-making, but hard to convert those principles into results. The real test of our values is not when things are going well, but when things are not going well. Political sensitivities, special-interest groups, stockholder expectations, time pressures, union demands, and competitive forces can derail principled decision-making. As a result, we sometimes bow to pressure and make expedient, short-term decisions. And those decisions frequently come back to haunt us. Today's "solutions," under those circumstances, frequently become tomorrow's problems.

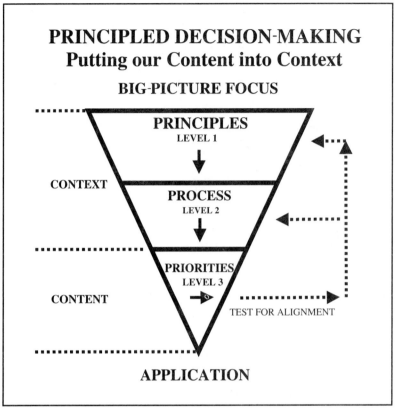

If leaders do not provide clear direction and make decisions consistent with that course, team members are forced to invent their own direction. Employees eventually lose sight of the overall corporate vision and values and begin making self-serving decisions. We-versus-they attitudes, low trust levels, budget games, hoarding materials, and poor work attitudes start creeping into the organization, and the customer eventually suffers from poor internal performance.

Principle-centered, value-driven companies integrate everything they do within the context of their philosophy. Who they are and what they do reflect the core ideologies within their carefully defined context of principles, process, and priorities. Note how the "Principled Decision-Making" triangle above illustrates the point.

Value-driven decisions require three levels of engagement:

Level 1 - Principles: The *"Guiding"* factors
- Mission: What is our purpose?
- Vision: Where are we going?
- Culture: What do we value?

Level 2 - Process: The *"Being"* factors
- How we function as a team.
- How we communicate.
- How we honor differences.
- How we support creativity.
- How we handle conflict.
- How we apply decision-making criteria.
- How we solve problems.

Level 3 - Priorities: The *"Doing"* factors
- Identifying priority issues.
- Exploring viable options.
- Solving problems creatively.
- Developing action plans.
- Implementing action plans.
- Evaluating results.

level 1: principles

This big-picture perspective provides a "navigational guide" to align mission, vision, and culture with team planning and decision-making. The guiding factors unite even diverse people behind a shared purpose and determine what we say "yes" to and what we say "no" to. These guiding principles provide a big picture context into which priorities can later be placed.

Teams often make a serious mistake by impatiently skipping principles and process to immediately address their priorities. On the surface, the team appears to have saved time by rapidly addressing the issue and pounding out a solution. Team members often feel good in getting "something tangible accomplished," only to later learn that the "solution" lacks ownership and commitment. In fact, team members often complain (in the parking lot) that their ideas were not listened to, that alternative solutions were not explored, and that overly directive leaders forced solutions upon them.

Over the long run, their "short-cut" approach ultimately consumes more time and resources as leaders now have to backtrack in an effort to open up communications, build trust, deal with strained interpersonal issues, and finally readdress the original issue. An old Native-American saying seems to capture the essence of this dilemma: *"Go slow—go fast. Go fast—go slow."*

"We need to learn to set our course by the stars,
not by the lights of every passing ship."

—Omar Bradley

---

level 2: process

This perspective emphasizes the "Being" elements: how the team interacts in addressing principles and issues. Level 2 focuses on the intangible, yet critical elements of fostering trust, supporting open communications, honoring differences, building a spirit of partnership, practicing win-win conflict methods, and enhancing creativity. Within Level 2, teams also benefit by taking the time to agree on appropriate problem-solving methods and decision-making criteria.

The pressure of time and the nature of some people to quickly pound out a solution often result in short-changing the value of process. Do not proceed to Level 3 until the team has a clear understanding of and commitment to the context of Levels 1 and 2. I am not advocating in any way that groups engage in analysis paralysis or engage in over-processing; these behaviors can be just as dysfunctional. Taking the time, however, to develop a shared context greatly facilitates addressing the actual issues and saves time in the long run.

level 3: priorities

This perspective ultimately addresses the actual task or "Doing" factors. In working through the issues, you have the context of Levels 1 and 2 to operate within. Making decisions within the framework of your principles and process greatly facilitates the creation of quality decisions while building unity of purpose and clarity of direction. In this stage, you and your team identify issues, explore options, participate in creative problem-solving, develop action plans, and explore appropriate follow-up and evaluation methods.

This systematic process of putting "content into context" challenges some hard-driving, action-oriented executives. They tend to quickly drop down to Level 3, priorities, and miss the benefit of Levels 1 and 2. They want the issues addressed and want results now, thank you. Although quick decisions are certainly appropriate in some situations, those rapid actions frequently result in long-term costs. The following experience demonstrates how a group of top executives learned how to put its content into context:

> *I received a phone call from the corporate president of a multibillion-dollar national corporation. He and five other leaders were "at war" with one another, causing chaos in the entire corporate environment. In addition to the corporate president,*

three regional presidents and two regional board chairmen participated in the organizational skirmish. Imagine how their infighting affected people further out in the organization!

I flew to their respective offices and met with each of the executives face to face. After listening to their tales of woe, I introduced to each of them the Principles-Process-Priority Triangle. Because their current approach clearly did not work, they demonstrated at least some openness to exploring decision-making alternatives.

To load the planned executive session for success, I sought out and secured two advance agreements from each of the six executives:

1. *That we would work through and come to agreement about the principles and process **before** addressing their priorities.*
2. *That if and when we ran into trouble while addressing their priorities, we would "pause," back up, and revisit our principles and process.*

Each of the executives bought into both of these agreements.

With these two agreements in hand, we flew to a common location and began our work, starting with principles. To their amazement, they achieved agreement about the big picture: the mission, vision, and culture or values. As we began exploring the Level 2 process of how we work together, how we communicate, how we handle conflict, and how we solve problems, these bottom-line-oriented executives started growing impatient. "Eric," they chimed, "we want to deal with our issues, not this process BS." "No," I responded, "you are not ready yet to address the issues in a way that produces a win-win result. You have had a lot of experience in battling over issues, and I don't want you to repeat that." I held firm, and they whined.

During a break, the six executives joined together in a "parking lot" meeting to grumble. As with the many times before, they wanted to jump into their issues and not deal with this "process BS*." (We are funny critters, we human beings. If something does not work, we tend to want to repeat it. These top executives were no exception to the rule.)*

Two things tend to unite people: a shared purpose or a common enemy. The executives now seemed united by a common enemy: me! They came in from the break and stated that they wanted to skip the process and address the issues. Can you imagine the pressure I felt coming from four presidents and two regional board chairmen to change the agenda?

I restated that we had an advance agreement to work through Levels 1 and 2 before addressing their priority topics and that they were not ready to deal with their issues. They had had plenty of experience dealing unsuccessfully with issues out of context, and I was not about to let them repeat that experience. "You gave me your word that we would experiment with this process," I responded, "and I am going to hold you to keeping your word." Seldom do people talk with top executives in this way. Somewhat stunned with my response, they half-heartedly agreed to stick to the original plan.

After working through the "process BS*," we finally started to address the issues they so impatiently wanted to deal with. Sure enough, they ran into trouble. Their old stuff surfaced and conflict once again stalled* *progress. But something different happened this time. One of the executives stated: "We need to pause right now and go back to Levels 1 and 2!" He even used the word **pause**. They collectively revisited their principles they had agreed to and the process tools we had implemented. Through their self-initiated correction, they reestablished a context to work within and then proceeded to revisit the issue they had stalled on moments before. It worked—and it worked well. Good for them!*

The executives learned the value of putting their content into context—and how to work back and forth between the principles, process, and priorities to achieve optimal results. They resolved their issues while continuing to build even stronger working relationships. The Bottom Line? They accomplished a corporate reorganization in less than five months—a task they expected to take 18 months. Not bad at all.

"Never succumb to pressure. Succumb only to principle."

—Roger Fisher & William Ury in *Getting to Yes!*

Linking principles and process with priorities in all corporate activities facilitates achieving tangible results while creating an environment that supports the spirit of partnership. Yes, leading by values takes more time initially, but functioning in a value-driven organization significantly diminishes such time-consuming activities as power struggles, guarding and expanding turf, political positioning, "CYA" memos and reports, and feeding the rumor mill.

In the long run, managing by values saves time, releases human potential, and focuses corporate resources on the more important issues. Amazing things happen when people work together in harmony toward a shared purpose and with common values. Paying attention to the "soft stuff" produces great bottom-line results while sharpening your competitive edge. Engaging your team first in the clarification of principles and process before dealing with your priorities generates significantly better results. And you can take those results to the bank!

"The measure of success
is not whether you have a tough problem to deal with,
but whether it's the same problem you had last year!"

—John Foster Dulles

Note what Ken Blanchard and Michael O'Connor have to say about the benefits of making value-based decisions on the facing page.

integrity: the foundation of long-term success

Organizations that do well in the long run commit to fundamental integrity their products, their services, and their process. They "walk their talk" even in the toughest of times. Those that mess with integrity generally pay a significant price internally with their employees and externally with their customers.

A medical-products company developed a sophisticated cardiac monitoring device that had significant promise for both patients and corporate stockholders. The research-and-development department (R&D) experienced considerable pressure from the chief executive officer to complete its work quickly so the device could be put into production and generate a return on investment for the stockholders.

The equipment, however, had a quirk that resulted in inaccurate readings under certain medical conditions. In spite of this disturbing, yet relatively rare quirk, the CEO continued to pressure

R&D to release the product for production. Against the better judgment of R&D executives, they yielded to pressure from the top. Although the cardiac monitor was a fine product overall, the quirk remained as they released it for production and distribution.

Strong sales of the product exceeded expectations and delighted stockholders. But The Bottom Line results soon reversed as physicians misdiagnosed patient after patient based on erroneous data from the equipment. Lawsuits came in from various parts of the country and dashed any hopes for strong profits. In addition to putting patients at risk, this breach of

 deliberate success gem

Managing by Values: Tennis Anyone?

Contributed by Kenneth Blanchard, Ph.D. & Michael O'Connor, Ph.D.

What kind of performance might a tennis, golf, or basketball player have if, instead of keeping his eyes on the ball, he always watched the scoreboard? Lots of companies seem to watch only their scoreboard (The Bottom Line). In doing so, they take their eyes off the ball (their relationships with people). When we keep our eye on consistently aligning business operations with our primary values, the scoreboard does, in fact, take care of itself!

The foundation of an effective organization is its purpose and values. An organization needs to know what it stands for and on what principles it will operate. With a clear picture of its purpose and values, an organization has a strong basis for evaluating its management practices and bringing them into alignment with this direction and philosophy.

Managing by values has three essential components:

1. Clarification of mission and values.
2. Communication of the mission and values.
3. Alignment of behavior with the values.

(cont.)

(cont. from p. 79) Unless employees both understand the values and can link them to their actual work lives, they're meaningless.

Do employees see the mission and values as guidelines they can identify with and which will create pride in the company? Do the mission and values truly provide a basis for making daily work decisions throughout the organization? Do they point toward a new set of rules of the road that will orient them when making management decisions, allocating resources, and solving technical and personnel problems? Or are we just watching the scoreboard?

Alignment is the heart and soul of managing by values. Once you have clarified your mission and values and communicated them to all your key stakeholders, then it's time to focus on your management practices to ensure they are consistent with your stated intentions, priorities, and performance goals. This process doesn't ignore the scoreboard. In fact, "walking the talk" on your mission and values positions employees, customers, and stockholders to achieve the best of scores.

—Kenneth Blanchard, Ph.D.
Coauthor of *The One-Minute Manager, Managing By Values,* and *Leadership By The Book*
www.blanchardlearning.com
—Michael O'Connor, Ph.D.
Coauthor of *The Platinum Rule* and *Managing By Values*

integrity put the company itself at financial risk.

This same chief executive officer that took shortcuts to the detriment of patients frequently talked about integrity as a company value. His value rhetoric had no substance. He succumbed to pressure rather than holding on to principle. Although the monetary cost of this integrity breach became significant, he also lost his credibility both within and outside of the company. People lost confidence in his leadership, and he lost his job.

In contrast to the experience you just read about, Hewlett-Packard's ink-jet printer division in Vancouver, Washington, experienced a rare problem with one of its products in early 1995. Only a small percentage of the machines it produced experienced the malfunction, and the glitch would likely surface long after the warrantee expired. Given the low probability of experiencing product failure and the likelihood that this would have occurred after expiration of the warranty, many companies would have passed this problem on to the customer. Not Hewlett-Packard. Instead, HP halted production and corrected the problem. Customers who had already received the ink jet printers were sent replacement parts for easy installation in their units—long before customers even knew of the potential problem.

"This above all: to thine own self be true,
and it must follow as the night the day,
thou canst not then be false to any man."

—William Shakespeare

Although the short-term costs to HP were high, the long-term value of building customer confidence in its products and enhancing employee pride in their company produced the kind of results that has enabled HP to do so well for many decades. At the time HP issued a news release regarding the product malfunction, I was considering the purchase of a sophisticated fax machine. I had narrowed my decision down to two quality brands: HP and one of its competitors. Because Hewlett-Packard had demonstrated such high integrity in standing behind its products, its actions persuaded me to buy the HP model. Business is built one customer at a time—and HP understands that principle. When values and behaviors are in harmony, integrity results. Alignment of actions with values is the difference that makes a difference.

"Circumstances do not determine a man, they reveal him."

—James Allen

How you respond to adverse conditions tests your values and sends strong messages to both your employees and customers. Consider Johnson & Johnson's response to the product-tampering incident of the early 1980s. As you may recall, someone tainted Tylenol with cyanide, resulting in seven deaths in the Chicago area. Johnson & Johnson acted swiftly to remove all its Tylenol products from retail shelves throughout the nation. This decision reportedly cost the company in excess of $100 million, but its actions maintained, if not increased, public confidence in their products. Johnson & Johnson was unwilling to trade its integrity for profits. Although the company took a significant, short-term financial hit, positive long-term results have continued to benefit the company and the customers it serves.[9, 10]

Several recent studies have concluded that companies functioning with integrity enjoy greater long-term profits than those not having or not following a strong set of business ethics. The Center of Ethics at Arizona State University completed a study of companies that consistently paid dividends for the past 100 years. Each of these companies practiced high ethical standards and recognized that service to the customer was fundamental to their long-term success.

Collins and Porras, in their book, *Built To Last,* studied companies that have been exceptionally successful for 50 years or more. Each of these companies has a strong culture founded in fundamental values that honor people, whether the employee or the customer, and build integrity into both its products and its way of doing business.

Mortimer Feinberg, in his book *Corporate Bigamy,* reported the findings of his interviews with the top 100 executives of the Fortune 500 companies. When asked, "What is necessary to go to the top and stay there?" honesty, character, and integrity were the overwhelming responses. Going to and staying at the top requires functioning with integrity. Feinberg's work was corroborated by a UCLA graduate management school survey of 1,300 corporate leaders. In that study, 71 percent ranked integrity at the top of 16 traits necessary for long-term success. Ranked at the bottom on that same list were appearance, popularity, formal business training, and conforming.

Maintaining the standards of stated values remains a challenge, even for peak performing companies. Jack Welch, recently retired chairman and CEO of General Electric, transformed the company he inherited in 1981. The task was not easy, and it is not complete. It's an ongoing process of balancing the creative tension between pragmatism and idealism. Aligning core ideology with all aspects of business focuses on a delicate balance of what Jack Welch referred to as "numbers and values." In an internal memo to GE corporate officers, Welch stated:

> *We don't have the final answer here—at least I don't. People who make the numbers and share our values go onward and upward. People who miss the numbers and share our values get a second chance. People with no values and no numbers—easy call. The problem is with those who make the numbers but don't share the values....We try to persuade them; we wrestle with them; we agonize over these people.*[11]

Value decisions are not easy, and even the best of companies struggles with them. In the struggle, however, clarity often emerges. Another company I am familiar with also wrestled with "numbers and values." One vice president of the most profitable division in the company clearly produced the numbers, but at significant expense to The Human Element. Although his return on investment (ROI) and profitability numbers were significantly higher than the other divisions, this vice president terrorized people. Turnover, grievances, and sick-leave statistics also set company records. Both his colleagues and his employees feared his wrath. Creativity and risk-taking plummeted as people protected themselves.

In a meeting with other top executives about company values, he stated, *"I am sick and tired of all this 'love thy neighbor' BS. I produce, and that's what counts."* The president had coached this vice president about his tyrannical behavior on numerous occasions. Confronted with a choice point of reinforcing corporate values or permitting this flesh-eating tyrant to continue his behaviors, the president invited the vice president into his office after the meeting—and gave him his final check.

putting values to work: southwest airlines

Leaders who give substance to values shape the corporate culture and create a value-driven organization that converts words into tangible results. Because of the consistent and remarkable results that Southwest Airlines achieves, I wanted to learn more. So I spent a few days at their corporate office exploring and experiencing their culture. They emphasized that Positively Outrageous Service (POS) results from treating people with respect and dignity—internally and externally. Honoring employees, celebrating their successes and contributions, creating a fun and energizing work environment, and encouraging employees to assume ownership and responsibility has resulted in Southwest Airlines' producing great bottom-line results. Every aspect of its culture promotes customer service.

Upon entering its corporate headquarters in Dallas, four items immediately caught my attention. Each of these made bold statements about their culture and how much they value employees:

1. "triple crown award"

Within feet of the front entrance, a trophy case prominently displayed the "Triple Crown Award." For five consecutive years, the U.S. Department of Transportation awarded Southwest Airlines with having the fewest customer complaints, best baggage handling, and best on-time performance.

Having won the Triple Crown for four consecutive years, Herb Kelleher, Chairman of Southwest, challenged the employees to make it five in a row. Herb tapped into Southwest's "Warrior Spirit" that had so successfully moved the airline through prior challenges. He promised employees that casual wear would be permanent at Southwest if they successfully met the five-year challenge. Additionally, the interior of a Southwest plane would be painted to include the names of all Southwest employees.

A "Gimme 5" campaign immediately sprung up as employees accepted the challenge. Today Southwest employees wear casual clothing, and a special Southwest airplane has all of their names inscribed in the interior.

2. the "people department."

Southwest honors people, whether passengers or employees, and it shows in everything they do. Off to the left of the main lobby, a "People Department" sign welcomes applicants into cheerful surroundings. Even a popcorn machine announces its presence with the fresh smell of hot-buttered popcorn available to staff and applicants.

Not your typical "human resources" department, the Southwest environment emphasized festive, friendly, and fast service—similar to its flights. Its "hire for attitude, train for skill"

philosophy manifests itself in every aspect of the physical surroundings and in its operations. A Southwest "People Department" executive said to me: *"We consider everyone we hire to
be a leader."*

3. herb's message

Herb Kelleher consistently demonstrates the value of honoring employees and understands the impact engaged employees
have on customer service. A large sign in the main lobby prominently displays Herb's message:

> *"The people of Southwest Airlines are the creators
> of what we have become—and of what we will be.*
>
> *Our people transformed an idea into a legend.
> That legend will continue to grow only so long as it
> is nourished—by our people's indomitable spirit,
> boundless energy, immense goodwill, and burning
> desire to excel.*
>
> *Our thanks—and our love—to the people of South-
> west Airlines for creating a marvelous family and won-
> drous airline."*

4. the personal touch

Having been in numerous corporate offices throughout the
country, I typically see a few select, large professional photographs of serious-looking corporate executives and board members. It's almost as if their eyes follow you as you walk down the
hall.

As with most things at Southwest, however, things are different at its corporate headquarters. Photographs of employees,
their families, and even their pets covered hallway walls throughout the corporate office. One full-time employee frames and

mounts photographs of employees and Southwest celebrations. Everywhere you look, you see the spirit of the Southwest with bright eyes and smiling faces.

Some might dismiss this emphasis on the personal touch as frivolous. Take another look, however. By treating the "internal customers" as number one in their culture, Southwest Airlines has enjoyed more than three decades of consecutive profitability, earned the most-favored airlines ranking by passengers, and earned placement in the top-four corporate rankings as the employer of choice. Are you ready to accept the challenge of treating your employees as "number one?"

putting values to work: the public sector

Snohomish County, in the state of Washington, provides a public-sector example of putting organizational values to work. Numerous groups of leaders and staff participated in a systematic value clarification process to identify their five core values: respect, partnership, service, integrity, and accountability.

Although it's still in the early phases of the organizational transformation process, Bob Drewel, the County Executive, introduced an employee- and management-development program titled "Values at Work: Essential Skills for Public Service." Drewel emphasized that *"our values are a reflection of the many thousands of distinct and tangible behaviors each of us is accountable for each day."* The mission, vision, value, and goal statements are more than inspirational in purpose. *"If used properly to guide our actions and decisions,"* according to Drewel, *"this document is our living guide—our litmus test for evaluating ideas and actions. In fact, our values are really nothing more than the sum total of all or our actions."*

Drewel conducted scores of meetings with leadership and staff to explore tangible methods of implementing the core values.

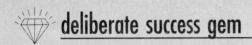

deliberate success gem

Values Speak
Louder Than Words

Contributed by Steve Van Andel

A return to traditional American family values has been the subject of headlines, best-selling books, political speeches, and discussions by concerned citizens across the country. At Quixtar, values are not a trend; they are a tradition. Values are a foundation of our success and a key to the effective leadership throughout Quixtar.

Jay Van Andel and Rich DeVos, cofounders of Amway (now reinvented as Quixtar), inspire more than two million people around the world to keep the hope alive that they can realize their dreams through a Quixtar business of their own. The Quixtar leaders have always role-modeled values—never demanding respect, but gaining respect by showing their respect for each Quixtar Independent Business Operator (IBO), regardless of his or her level of success.

Growing up in the Amway business, I saw that Rich and Jay did not leave their values at home when they went to the office every day or into the community. The values, instilled by their parents, were practiced consistently **(cont.)**

Through this process, he built awareness of and commitment to the values. Tangible applications of the values were explored in the context of both The Bottom Line and The Human Element. In addition to emphasizing the values in strategic planning and everyday operations, Drewel implemented a six-year process of value integration. Additionally, Drewel encouraged each employee to develop his or her personal mission and value statements to enhance individual life experiences.

The principle-centered, value-driven changes in Snohomish County are beginning to make a difference internally. Even former critics of local government notice the changes. Community organizations are now inviting Snohomish County leaders to conduct seminars on how to shape the culture through implementation of vision and values. Local high schools have invited Snohomish County leaders to work with graduating seniors to explore how to find employment in principle-centered organizations. The changes are contagious.

Integration of the values into the soul of the organization is a long-term process. Drewel stated, *"We want a culture based on trust, wherein we celebrate our differences while becoming a customer-focused, principle-centered, peak-performing organization."* As guideposts that lead the organization to its mission and vision, the values are taking on

(**cont. from p. 88**) every day and everywhere. These fundamental values have transcended change and continue as the business progressed into its next phase of e-commerce development: Quixtar.

The Quixtar leadership succeeded through hard work, self-reliance, and persistence. Those values are instilled in all Quixtar IBOs in building their own businesses. The compassion Quixtar leaders demonstrated, by sharing their success with their community, is reflected by Quixtar IBOs who've raised millions of dollars for Easter Seals and daily help others fulfill their dreams. Their friendship and partnership of more than a half a century is the foundation of the IBO partnerships that are essential to the success of Quixtar.

The cofounders have a loyal following because they've led by **keeping their promises** to Quixtar IBOs. They've motivated IBOs through countless speeches to tens of thousands of people over the decades. But, in the end, what they've done speaks more loudly than words.

—Steve Van Andel
Chairman, Quixtar Corporation
www.quixtar.com

significant meaning. *"The direction of the ship has changed,"* according to Drewel, *"and we want each of you to be on board."*

Another client of mine, a large acute care hospital in the Midwest, likewise developed a core set of values that continues to shape the way it provides services. Also through an extensive and participative process, the medical center identified four core values: respect, integrity, service, and excellence. Not just words on a piece of paper, these core values guide policy formation, strategic planning, decision-making, leadership and staff development, and the hiring of new associates. Additionally, a systematic coaching process integrates the core values into the development and assessment of associates to guide their progress consistent with the mission and vision of the medical center.

Measurable gains have been achieved in patient satisfaction, market share increase, a surplus of revenues over expenses, and employee fulfillment. The drive for excellence in all levels of the medical center goes far beyond the rhetoric experienced in many "wannabe" organizations—the drive for technical and human element excellence is a way of life at the medical center.

"To make the right choices in life, you have to get in touch with your soul. To do this, you need to experience solitude, which most people are afraid of, because in the silence you hear the truth and know the solutions."

—Deepak Chopra, M.D.

Corporate culture reflects what you say "yes" to and what you say "no" to. Actions always speak louder than words. Take a look at your collective decisions and actions. What are they communicating to others about what is really important? What values are you supporting and promoting within your corporate culture? If people caught your attitudes and behaviors (which they will), what impact will that have within your circle of influence—your work and your family? What does your culture demonstrate about the importance of customers? Because your culture defines who you are, pay attention to the messages you are sending.

chapter 6

sustaining a customer-focused culture

the rules have changed!

"Profit is the applause you get for satisfying customer needs and creating a fulfilling work environment."

—Ken Blanchard

THE DAYS OF merely satisfying customers are over. Customers expect far more. Peak-performing organizations recognize this fundamental shift in customer expectations and integrate it into every aspect of their culture the philosophy of delighting customers. From the CEO to the newly hired entry-level employee, serving the customer is a way of life, as the following experience demonstrates.

The Salish Lodge, in the State of Washington, seemed like a great place to facilitate a strategic-planning retreat for a particular corporate client. The lodge has excellent conference facilities, a reputation for outstanding service, and a pleasant environment to encourage creative thinking.

By the end of the second day, my client had generated numerous ideas regarding its new vision and core strategies. I volunteered to take all of its rough-draft flip-chart papers to my hotel room that evening to synthesize the ideas into a more user-friendly format for our final planning day. With that intention in mind, I removed all of the flip-chart papers from the conference room walls and stacked them on the floor to await my return from dinner.

After dinner, I entered our conference room to retrieve the charts. Consistent with my experience at the Salish Lodge, the conference room had already been cleaned and meticulously prepared for the following day. The peak-performing housekeeping department had completed its work with thoroughness and attention to detail—except for one thing! It assumed that the flip charts on the floor were intended for disposal. The charts, representing two solid days of strategic planning work with corporate executives, had been trashed. And the housekeeping staff had already gone home. I was in deep doo-doo.

Fortunately, I could recall most of my client's ideas and was able to prepare the synthesized version for its consideration the next day. I always, however, want to work off of its documents and to have those present for comparative purposes. Obviously, this was not an option.

The following morning, I arrived early to get things set up in the conference room for the final strategic planning day. A Salish Lodge catering employee also arrived early to set up the coffee and continental breakfast. I talked with her about the problem I experienced with the missing charts. Clearly understanding the significance of the issue, she looked me in the eye and said, "I'll take care of it." Something in her voice gave me a ray of hope.

When the executives arrived, I explained the situation to them and apologized. Although they understood, no one was happy with the circumstances, especially considering the significance of the missing data.

Thirty minutes into our conference, the same catering employee arrived through the back door of the conference room and unobtrusively whispered to me: "I have your charts!" Not only had she climbed into the large trash bin at the back of the hotel to find and retrieve my charts, but she ironed them!

After placing the charts on a table in the back of the room, she started to leave. I said to her, "Wait a minute. Come up here! Every time we have asked you and others here at the Salish Lodge for something, you always exceed our expectations. Tell us about that."

At that point, this entry-level employee gave my executive clients a 10-minute presentation about the customer-focused culture at the Salish Lodge. After first stating that "we are particular about who we hire," she went on to describe their mission and values, their commitment to bringing out the best of every employee, and how their culture supports serving customers at the highest level.

My top executive clients sat in awe as they listened to a new employee, who had been with the Salish Lodge only four months, effectively demonstrate and communicate its mission, values, and customer-service commitment. At that point, the corporate president said to me, "What do we need **you** for? We have **her!**"

Organizations achieving deliberate success integrate customer service into their culture and empower employees to do and be their best. When one of your employees is put to the test—such as the catering associate at the Salish Lodge—how well will she perform? Because employees reflect what leaders value, what messages are your employees getting about the importance of customer service?

customer service: the rules have changed

"If you don't take care of your customers, somebody else will."

—Ken Blanchard

Everything—well, almost everything—in business seems to be changing. Product life, customer expectations, product delivery methods, technology, global competition, and the list goes on. Some surprising changes are also happening. Several of the most sacred "rules" related to customer service are now obsolete, and your business needs to be tuned in to the new rules. For example:

- The Old Rule: "Customers want to be *satisfied.*"
- The New Rule: "Customers expect to be *delighted.*"

- The Old Rule: "The customer is Number One."
- The New Rule: "The employees are Number One."

- The Old Rule: "The customer is always right."
- The New Rule: "Some customers should be fired."

These new rules fundamentally change the way you do business, and if you don't pay attention and sharpen your competitive edge, your competitors will likely edge you out. Remember the days when merely satisfying customers resulted in long-term business relationships? No longer can you count on *satisfied* customers, however, for return business. In fact, an increasing number of satisfied customers aren't returning at all. They are leaving for your competitors! Why? The rules have changed. Expectations have risen far beyond mere satisfaction; customers now expect to be *delighted!* Customers now seek significantly higher value than they settled for in the past. Being good doesn't cut it anymore. Your whole organization—that means everybody— needs to focus on providing *great* service.

Customers themselves are getting more discriminating and more demanding. In this highly competitive market, they have an increasing number of options from which to purchase products and services. Customer loyalty, the old standby, lasts about as long as your kid's melting ice cream cone on a hot summer day. At this very moment, your competitors are seeking ways to attract your customers with better service, quicker delivery time, higher quality products, Internet transactions, home delivery, lower costs, personalized attention, and better results. Are you up to the challenge?

The cost of generating a new client ranges from five to eight times the cost of retaining an existing client. If a company spends $10 million on marketing efforts and sales promotions to attract new customers, it would wisely invest at least $2 million to keep its present customers.[12] Marriott Hotels considers this just good business by hiring the right people, budgeting generously for people development, and investing in a culture that supports customer service. J. Willard Marriott, Jr., Chief Executive of Marriott Hotels, accepts clear accountability for generating a customer service environment. *"My job,"* he says, *"is to motivate them, teach them, help them, and care about them."*[13]

Because the rules have changed—and will continue to change— your business success depends on delivering innovative products and services in innovative ways. In a Tom Peters seminar I attended, he said, *"People need banking services, but they don't need banks."* Look around; it seems that everyone is getting into the "banking business." My neighborhood Safeway grocery store has a Wells Fargo "branch office" next to the checkout line. My stockbroker now offers more banking services at greater convenience than my former bank. Internet banking services are available 24 hours a day, and I don't have to wait in line or even lick stamps. It seems that people don't really need banks at all. Perhaps your customers don't even need your business—at least in its current form.

A major law firm that is a client of mine discovered three somewhat painful ways in which the rules are changing: One, its major corporate clients are setting the legal fees they will pay, two, a number of their clients are now providing their own in-house lawyers, and three, new competitors are arising from unanticipated sources, including the expanding "legal" services provided by accounting firms and CPAs and the growing involvement of mediation consultants.

Whether in banking, lawyering, or manufacturing, new competitors show up on the scene from both expected and unexpected sources. Customers demand a greater say in the design, quality, delivery, and cost of products and services. Clients are beginning to act more like "business partners" than traditional customers of the past. Service is all about developing and nurturing a conscious, consistent, and caring connection with your customers. Stay in touch with your customers, and they will stay in touch with you.

"We pay too much attention to prospects and not enough attention to customers."

—Tom Peters

dissatisfied customers usually leave silently

Why do customers leave? Both the Forum Corporation and the Technical Assistance Research Program (TARP) reached essentially the same conclusions: 15 percent of customers leave because of finding a better product and 15 percent leave because of finding a cheaper product. The most significant factor, however, relates to the human element: 70 percent switch to a competitor because of a lack of individual attention or because the moment of contact was so poorly handled. A significant majority of customers leave because of one bad experience with one employee.

The average business never hears from 96 percent of its unhappy customers; they leave in silence. Those who do complain, however, are more likely to do repeat business—especially if the company listens and quickly responds to their complaints. For every complaint received, according to the TARP consumer-behavior study, there are 26 (six of which are serious) who will never tell you of their distress. To your detriment, however, they will tell others about their negative experience—for years and years later. How well are you l-i-s-t-e-n-i-n-g to your customers and effectively responding to their needs?

Have you ever stopped doing business with a company because of one bad experience with one of its employees—one "moment of truth" that went astray? Consistent with consumer-behavior statistics, I also tend to tell others about those experiences. This personal experience demonstrates my point:

While driving home from a leadership workshop I conducted in Seattle, I stopped for gas at a "service" station in Olympia. The station had just recently installed new self-service gas pumps that accept the customer's credit card—standard procedure for many people. In my own home state of Oregon, however, attendants fill your tank, so I was unfamiliar with the routine. It seemed simple enough, however—just three easy steps complete with pictures on the pump to guide me through the process. I inserted my credit card into the appropriate slot, but the pump did not activate. After checking to see that I inserted the card correctly, I repeated the procedure. Again, the pump did not activate. I checked to make sure that the black stripe on the credit card was in the right position, and repeated the process.

At this point, I felt a bit frustrated and a little dumb. Within moments, a booming voice over the public address system stated, "Person on pump number 11, you have your card in backwards." Where was this voice coming from? And surely they were not talking to me. I looked up only to discover that I was at pump number 11. Other customers looked my way with smirks on their faces; they knew I was from Oregon and couldn't figure out how to pump my own gas. I felt even dumber and more than slightly embarrassed.

I reread the simple instructions, studied the three pictures designed for illiterates, and less confidently reinserted my credit card. No luck. Then the booming voice returned on the PA system: "Person on pump number 11, come into the office. You are doing it all wrong!"

Basically, I am a peaceful person. Yet, I was now on a hunt. Into the station I go to find a 21-year-old kid standing behind a microphone at the counter. He thought he was hot stuff. I momentarily forgot all the principles I teach about win-win conflict, pausing, seeking first to understand, and listening. I was mad. Even though he was much bigger than I was, I wanted to deck him! I didn't need to have a PA system to get his full attention as I boomed to him, "Don't you ever speak to me or any customer that way!" Although I momentarily felt better, he, of course, did not get my point.

Without apologizing for his poor customer-service tactics, he then ordered a young coworker to accompany me to the pump and show me how to use the system. She and I shuffled back to the infamous pump number 11, with all eyes following us. She inserted my card properly into the pump, and it didn't work! The pump had a malfunction! I was doing it right all along! Yes!

Do you think I will ever go back to that service station? Not on your life! Even if I were out of gas and had to walk miles past that station to get to the next, I would do it.

Customer feedback is a gift! Make it easy for your customers to share their concerns, and train your associates to listen, listen, listen. Procter & Gamble has a toll-free customer service hotline to facilitate and encourage customers to unload their complaints. Given the huge range and volume of products P&G produces, the company receives a significant number of customer complaints: more than 200,000 per year.

P&G loves to hear from its customers—even those who complain. L-i-s-t-e-n-i-n-g to the input of customers continues to be an exceptional source of innovative ideas for new product development. And it's simply good business to stay connected with valued customers.

deliberate success gem

Customers: Adapting to a New Relationship

Contributed by Peter Block, Ph.D.

We have awakened to the existence of customers, but only barely. Customers want a unique response. They want us to make an exception in response to the specifics of their requirements. Customer service runs deeper than friendliness, listening skills, and a positive attitude.

Customers want more control over the relationship with us. They want to choose who serves them; they want influence over the terms of the sale; they want choice in the way the product or service is delivered; they want one contact person, even though their answer may require the cooperation of four different departments.

Can an organizational structure that demands control, consistency, and predictability deliver, on a timely basis, the highly adaptive responses to clients who require greater and greater choices over where and how to get their needs met? I think not. A consistent response to a customer will no longer insure our survival. Customers want a unique response to their requirements.

—Peter Block, Ph.D.
Author of *Stewardship* and
The Empowered Manager
www.peterblock.com

"Dissatisfied customers," according to Peter Block, *"teach us how to do business."* Block also challenges us to consider that people who do not use our services teach us how to sell and that other departments that are angry with us teach how to improve our product, our service, and the way that we work with them. The very thing that you resist hearing usually contains within it your greatest learning opportunity. Listen, listen, listen. Then respond in a way that exceeds their expectations. By so doing, you build trust, confidence, and customer loyalty. Your genuine attentiveness will keep customers coming back.

customers don't want what they say they want!

Customers are funny sometimes: They usually don't tell you what they *really* want. A customer comes into a hardware store, for example, and asks for a drill. He doesn't want a drill; he wants a hole! Once tool manufacturers learned that customers didn't want drills, R&D folks developed creative new products that made holes! And sales increased.

A customer doesn't want the life and disability insurance for which she pays big bucks. What does she actually want? Peace of mind. Insurance companies that think they are in the business of selling policies will soon become extinct in this competitive market.

Customers are not really interested buying your products or services. They don't want your drills and they don't want your insurance policies. They want a *result* that benefits them. They want to be delighted by what your products and services will do for them. And they want to be delighted by your personalized, innovative, accessible service. It's just that simple!

A manufacturing client of mine thought it was in the business of selling its underground trucks and scoops to mines throughout the world. I asked, *"What if someone invented a way of getting the ore out of the ground faster and cheaper than using your trucks and scoops. Would your customers continue to buy your trucks and scoops?"* The response was a clear *"no!"*

The company realized that those big, wonderful yellow trucks and scoops it manufactured were not what the customers really wanted. As a result, it made a fundamental shift in even its company mission that now reads to "enhance the profitability and productivity of our customers by providing superior mining products, innovative solutions, and quality services." Not just words on a piece of paper, this fundamental shift positions the company to constantly focus on providing innovative products and highly valuable services to its customers. This shift ultimately enhances the profitability of their own company and the profitability of the customers it serves.

Bob Farrell opened his first highly successful Farrell's Ice Cream Parlor in Portland, Oregon, in 1963. Focusing on superior customer service and having fun, he grew the business to 55 stores before selling his ice-cream kingdom to the Marriott Hotels only 10 years later. What was the foundation of his success? *"I didn't sell ice cream,"* Farrell said of his years with the ice cream parlors in the *Oregonian* in August 1998. *"I sold a good time. Ice cream was the vehicle."*

According to Jay Abrahams, the $3,000-per-hour marketing consultant, the greater, the clearer, and the more powerful you are at expressing, articulating, demonstrating, illustrating, and comparing how you render that advantage better than anybody else, the more business you get. Customers are buying a result, a benefit, or an outcome that serves their needs and interests. *"The only reason people do business with a company,"* according to Abrahams, *"is that they see an advantage in it for themselves."* Your job, then, is to make sure that every aspect of your corporate culture aligns with and exceeds the changing expectations of your customers.

the 6 great expectations of customers

Sharpening your competitive edge requires staying in tune with what your customers currently value and with their changing interests. Pay attention to what you can do to not only add value to the customer, but also to create value where it did not exist before. Businesses will purchase your products or services if they increase their profits, their productivity, their market share, or their competitive position. Customers are purchasing *results* and the way in which those results provide value to them.

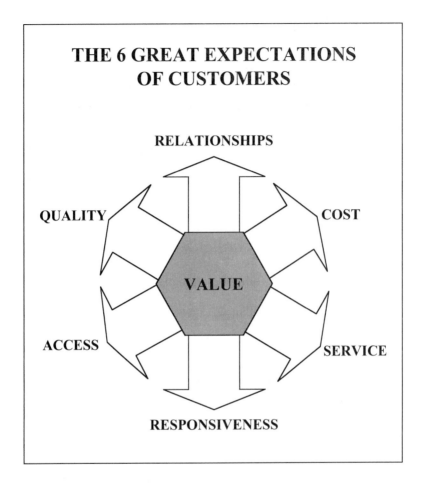

THE 6 GREAT EXPECTATIONS OF CUSTOMERS

RELATIONSHIPS

QUALITY

COST

VALUE

ACCESS

SERVICE

RESPONSIVENESS

Although you may be interested in a sale, they are interested in value.

You cannot assume that you know how they define value; you have to be on speaking terms with them! What one customer highly values may not even register on another customer's radar screen. Tuning in to those differences and doing a class-act job of meeting those needs will make you the customer's provider of choice.

Customers seek value, benefits, and results from your services and products. Even as you read these words, your known

and perhaps unknown competitors are actively seeking to provide even higher value to your customers. Your *commercial customers* are actively looking to enhance their productivity and
profitability. To what extent are you meeting—or exceeding—
their needs? Your *retail customers* are seeking some form of
pleasure or peace of mind. To what extent are you meeting these
interests? Your *internal customers* expect quality, completed
work from you to make their job easier and more fulfilling. How
do you measure up?

Customer value is a function of six key elements:

1. Cost.
2. Service.
3. Access.
4. Responsiveness.
5. Relationships.
6. Quality.

Through the eyes of your key customers, to what extent are
you viewed as providing high value with regard to each of these
key factors?

1. cost

Although cost is not always the sole criteria for making a
purchasing decision, cost-conscious customers very closely monitor your pricing structure. And they seem to be increasingly less
loyal to established business relationships. In the past, you had
much more control regarding what you charged for your products and services. Now, the market in general and your customers in particular seem to be telling you what you can charge. For
example:

- Managed-healthcare companies determine what they
  will pay hospitals and physicians for their services.

- Major corporations set the level of compensation for the corporate lawyers they retrain.
- Informed buyers use the internet to make instant product-price comparisons on anything from caviar to computers to cars—and your prices better be competitive.

The rules have changed. Your customers, your competitors, and even third-party payers set the stage for you to drive costs and prices down. Are you sharpening your competitive pricing edge?

2. service

"What about your business," challenges Jay Abrahams, *"gives greater advantage, greater benefit, and greater result to your customer than your competitors?"* Why would a customer select you over another provider? How do you know for sure? At the conclusion of your interactions with a customer, ask, *"What can I do next time to make my services even more valuable in meeting your needs?"*

IBM has long identified "customer service" as one of its most important values. As you know, however, IBM ran into significant trouble during the late 1980s and early 1990s. It became complacent about "customer service" as its competitors claimed chunk after chunk of IBM's former market share. IBM finally responded to its corporate "wake-up call" through its "Back to Basics" initiative that refocused on the "customer service" value that had served the company so well for decade after decade. According to a *Business Week* article, the president of IBM now spends approximately 40 percent of his time staying connected with customers. IBM is back on track. How much time are you spending with your key customers?

3. access

"Location, location, location," a fundamental criterion for business success, takes on new meaning in today's global economy and e-commerce environment. The concept advocated by Tom Peters that *"people need banking services but not banks"* applies here. If you are locked into a certain way of making your business available, you are probably already in trouble—or soon will be! Customers want easy access to your services. If you make it tough for customers to get access to your products and services because of inconvenient location, obsolete systems, or rigid policies, your competitors will find a way to serve your former customers more effectively.

With easy Internet access and next-day delivery to the customer's door, your competitors may now be halfway around the world, yet only six-tenths of a second away in computer time. Easy access to products and services will continue to produce profits as busy customers seek instant results.

Electronic commerce and network marketing are transforming the form and function of serving customers. Amway reinvented itself to become Quixtar, an e-commerce–driven, multilevel marketing business that now provides easy Internet access to a vast array of goods and services while capitalizing on both "high tech and high touch." The exponential growth of network marketing and electronic commerce is a function of low transaction costs, high-tech distribution methods, prompt access to a wide range of products, and person-to-person business relationships. Thousands of small, independent business owners engage friends, associates, and others in user-friendly, e-commerce systems that move billions of dollars of products. No longer an alternative business practice, the "sleeping giant" of network marketing has awakened in Corporate America.

4. responsiveness

Responsiveness takes on two forms: actively seeking to delight a customer and quickly and effectively addressing customer complaints. In this increasingly competitive market, customers rapidly size up your ability to perform on both the "pleasers" and the "displeasers." The expectations of customers continue to rise, but their tolerance for mediocre performance has sharply declined.

"It's not my job." "It's against policy." "You will have to talk to my supervisor about that." How do you react when, as a customer yourself, you hear a disempowered employee make these kinds of statements to you? Instead of working through obstacles to meet your needs, he or she creates obstacles! Chances are that you will do business someplace else the next time around. The same goes for *your* customers.

You do not hear these disempowered statements at Nordstrom, Southwest Airlines, Disneyland, Les Schwab Tire Service, Johnson County Community College, or the Ritz Carlton Hotels. Peak-performing organizations understand that they are in business to provide something of value to their clients, and they empower their employees to do just that. In these organizations, leaders create a customer-focused culture and empower even front-line staff to serve the needs of customers.

You also need to have the courage to say "no" to your customers when appropriate. If you allow a customer to pressure you into making a promise you cannot keep, client relationships will suffer. Stay focused on the principle of "underpromise and overdeliver."

Even the best organizations, on the other hand, make mistakes. When they do, however, they respond quickly and effectively in correcting the situation. Let me share a story about an experience in a Ritz Carlton Hotel:

I was invited to be a keynote speaker on "Peak Performance" at a conference in Los Angeles. My client arranged for my wife and I to stay at a Ritz Carlton Hotel near Los Angeles International Airport. Staying in a class-act hotel brought a smile to my wife's face.

Everything about the service was impeccable—except for one flaw: After servicing our room one morning, housekeeping forgot to replenish the bathroom with towels and soap. Upon returning from breakfast, my wife noticed the discrepancy and asked me to take care of the situation. (I seem to have a "Honey-Do" list even when traveling.)

I called the concierge to advise her of the problem. She responded with an apology—not an excuse—and said she would take care of it immediately. Within minutes, a reassuring knock at our door signaled the arrival of fresh towels and other supplies. The problem was handled quickly and efficiently.

But at the Ritz Carlton, quick and efficient problem-resolution is not enough. Customer relations, in this company's culture, requires going beyond expectations. A few minutes later, another knock at our door sounded the arrival of the unexpected. This time, a stately man in a white uniform presented a silver tray of gourmet chocolates. A personal note from the concierge accompanied the chocolates and apologized for our inconvenience. Wow!

The staff couldn't have self-corrected more appropriately. My wife is a chocoholic! (She has authored the Chocolate For A Woman's Soul *series of books.) We then started looking around to see if we could find something else that was "wrong" with the Ritz Carlton in anticipation of how the staff might respond next time!*

Although several customer service rules have changed, one remains constant: "underpromise and overdeliver." In any organization, it's important to promise great service and deliver even greater service. Even when you make a mistake, the customer usually will stay with you if you respond quickly and with a touch of class. Thank you, Ritz Carlton Hotels, for reminding us of the importance of doing the basics—exceptionally well.

5. relationships

You don't need to be reminded of the importance of building positive customer relations. Yet, an amazing number of companies simply don't get it. And they pay a huge price for that insensitivity as their customers take a hike to their competitors.

Building positive customer relations just makes good business sense from a financial, friendship, and customer loyalty perspective. The following example demonstrates power of building solid business relationships:

> *A heavy equipment distributor I studied developed a unique "Profit Partnership," engaging the manufacturers, itself (as the distributor), and its retail customers. Several times a year and at his own expense, the distributor assembled top executives from the manufacturing and retailing companies to join him in exploring ways to improve customer service, enhance their products, refine their distribution and delivery systems, and increase their collective profits. This "Profit Partnership" created a safe forum to exchange innovative ideas for enhancing customer service, improving products, and generating higher profits. (The president of the distributing company understood the distinct benefit of tending to both The Bottom Line and The Human Element.)*

One of his retail customers experienced financial problems and could not make payments for the items it had purchased from the distributor. A typical business response to this dilemma would have been for the distributor to send out strongly worded collection letters, turn the account over to a collection agency, or even sue for damages.

This distributor, however, looked upon the financial crisis as an opportunity to build relationships while simultaneously enhancing profitability. Instead of taking action against his "Profit Partner," the distributor provided two of his most seasoned financial experts without cost to his financially troubled retailing partner. The two financial wizards spent several days in the retailer's business seeking ways to strengthen its financial position. The sound counsel of the experts paid off handsomely for the retailer, and the company started to turn a profit. As a result, the retailer paid off its debt to the distributor.

More importantly, however, the generous, sensitive, and professional manner in which the distributor handled the retailer's crisis solved the immediate financial problem and positioned it for long-term financial viability. Considering that a new customer costs from five to eight times more to attract than retaining an existing customer, the return on investment for working with this customer was nothing short of profound. In fact, that retailer continued to purchase the distributor's products long after a new competitor moved in with a foreign alternative that cost less and offered more features.

Building a solid business relationship, especially under difficult financial circumstances, created a customer for life! It doesn't get better than that!

Your customers do not want consistency—if that means being treated just like any other customer. They want you to recognize their uniqueness. Customers want you to make an exception when meeting their needs, they want more control in how you do business with them,[14] and they want to interact with someone who has the authority to deal with their needs and interests on the spot.

Arthur Blank, CEO of The Home Depot, reported in the January 24, 2000, issue of *Forbes, "We're in the relationship business, not the transaction business. People can buy this merchandise somewhere else. The challenge is always remembering to walk in our customers' footsteps, not in our own."* Keeping that focus on relationships contributed to the 250-fold increase in stock value since its first offering. Paying attention to the human element is smart business.

"The only thing that your competitors can't steal from you is your relationship with your competitors."

—Ken Blanchard

---

6. quality

"If you are not committed to being the best in your field," according to Brian Tracy, *"you are unconsciously accepting mediocrity. If you are not continually getting better, you are probably getting worse."* Sustaining your competitive edge requires that you continually enhance your products and services and that you

hold yourself accountable to produce world-class quality. To settle for anything less almost assures that your customers will walk.

At this very moment, your competitors are hard at work improving their products, enhancing their service, and refining their quality. Even your most "loyal" customers actively compare your prices, quality, and service with your competitors. How do you measure up? How long can you sustain that competitive advantage? How do you know?

Customers rightfully expect that you build quality into every aspect of your products and services and that you understand their changing interests. A number of industries have learned powerful and painful lessons by not paying sufficient attention to consumer interests. Detroit auto-makers lost a significant share of their market to foreign manufacturers who paid much closer attention to quality and innovation. Fortunately, Detroit is finally paying attention to their "wake-up call" and addressing the quality issues commanding attention.

Banks, hospitals, health-maintenance organizations, Internet service providers, home-builders, computer manufacturers, and perhaps even your company are getting the message that being "good" is simply not good enough. Sophisticated and discriminating customers clearly expect that you knock their socks off with legendary service and outrageous quality. If you don't, they will find a competitor who can perform. It's just that simple.

So, my friend, your customers don't want your products and services. They want something of value that those products and services represent. They want to increase productivity, to enhance profits, or to experience some form of pleasure or peace of mind. When you do a particularly good job of providing consistently high value, you can take the results to the bank!

customers count—both of them!

A customer is defined as anyone who receives your work. You have, then, *two* important customers: your traditional, external customer and your fellow associates, or internal customers. Delighting both your internal and external customers becomes the benchmark for sustaining peak performance and sharpening your competitive edge. Many of us have been taught that the external customer comes first. This is not necessarily so! Marriott Hotels supports a philosophy that the employee comes first, the customer second, and the stockholder third. When employees are treated particularly well, they will likely treat the guests particularly well. When that happens, count on the guest returning—thus making the stockholder happy. Paying attention to The Human Element can and does have a favorable impact on The Bottom Line.

The output of one team becomes the input for another team. We need to assure that the handoff between teams is as smooth, quick, and efficient as a relay runner passing the baton on to the next runner. In track events, relay runners pay careful attention to the handoff. The speed and effectiveness of the handoff often makes the difference between a winning or losing race.

One of the key roles of a leader or coach is to facilitate horizontal relationships and interactions ("handoffs") between functions and departments. Rather than focusing on traditional vertical relationships, the "coach" now coordinates activities, opens channels of communication, removes interdepartmental obstacles, cuts red tape, and does away with barriers to creativity. The coach engages in activities to facilitate intra- and interdepartmental handoffs.

In a reengineering workshop I attended with Michael Hammer, author of *The Reengineering Revolution,* he likened interdepartmental turf to old fiefdoms—complete with castles and motes. Many departments perform their functions within castlelike isolation, and, according to Hammer, "catapult" their completed work over the wall onto the turf of the next castle. This next group performs some function on the project and catapults it on to the following group, and so on until the product is eventually completed. All the while, Hammer claims that each fiefdom protects its turf rather than coordinates, withholds rather than communicates, and hides rather than shares. It's amazing that anything can get done under those circumstances. A high price tag and questionable quality often accompany these dysfunctional activities.

Delighting both our internal and external customers must remain a high priority to achieve productive and profitable results. The same principles of serving external customers apply to serving internal customers. Tear down the walls. Get rid of the turf. Build bridges. Create synergy. Build a culture that honors, supports, and sustains what Ken Blanchard appropriately describes as *"legendary customer service."*

> *The finance department in one of my client organizations had a clear, yet unstated mission: "Catch other departments doing something wrong!" They considered themselves to be the organizational cops and auditors. Other departments lived in fear of these self-appointed financial police. Managers throughout the organization creatively worked around the finance department and hid any information that the financial cops might use against them.*

> *The folks in the finance department, on the other hand, complained about "them"—their internal customers from operations who paid little attention to budgeting, forecasting, and financial analysis. For some reason, the operational managers seemed highly uncooperative. Obviously, the finance department did not get it!*

After years of poor financial performance and sustained combat with their internal customers, the financial gurus decided to so something differently. Rather than fighting with their internal customers, the financial cops mustered up the courage to look at themselves.

In a planning and team-development workshop I facilitated with the finance department, we revisited their mission and the outcomes they sought to achieve in the organization. What did they want? They wanted managers to drive out excess costs and generate new revenue opportunities. They wanted operational managers to skillfully use the financial data available and to call upon the technical expertise of the finance department. They wanted all levels of managers to consciously and willingly participate in creating sustained profitability and financial health. In short, they wanted the operational managers to function in a spirit of partnership to achieve financial viability.

I challenged the financial experts to explore "if you don't like what you are getting back, take a look at what you are putting out." They wanted partnership, yet they functioned as financial cops. That does not compute! They got the point and began a new journey that significantly revised their mission, their culture, and customer service values.

Their new mission reads: "In the spirit of partnership, trust, and open communication, our mission is to assure the long-term profitability and fiscal viability of (our company) while functioning as financial consultants and resources to our internal customers." They consciously shifted their own focus to be "95 percent consultant and only 5 percent cop." What a difference!

The paradigm shift from "cop" to "consultant" oc-curred in both spirit and practice. But they had a terrible internal reputation. In an effort to assist their internal cus-tomers see them differently—very differently—they formed a kazoo band and marched unannounced into each of the departments they served to demonstrate their newly learned musical talents! They proudly announced their new mission and committed to being of service as finan-cial consultants to their operational partners. Not stop-ping there, the newly self-appointed "financial consult-ants" met individually with their operational partners to explore how they could be of service.

Things began to happen—good things! Trust be-gan to build. Instead of hiding their financial concerns, operational managers began to expose their financial vulnerabilities and look to the financial consultants as important resources. This conscious shift in both their ways of "Being" (The Human Element) and "Do-ing" (The Bottom Line) began to produce positive and productive results in enhancing the overall fiscal health of the organization.

"Life is simultaneously a journey, a destination, and a state of being."

—T.S. Eliot

---

some customers should be fired!

Customers are not always right, and leaders need to have the courage to support the mission, vision, and values of their own organizations—even if it results in "firing" a customer. Some years ago, I interviewed the general manager of the Hard Rock Cafe in

New York City. His highly profitable restaurant emphasizes "being of service, but not servants to" its customers. If a customer treats an employee poorly, that customer is invited to leave.

At Southwest Airlines, Chairman Herb Kelleher responded to a series of complaint letters from a particular passenger who wanted assigned seating and something other than peanuts for dinner. His message to her was *"we will miss you!"*[15] Kelleher recognized that Southwest Airlines cannot be true to its mission by being all things to all people.

"Firing" an external customer, obviously, requires great thought and care. To prevent this difficult situation from arising in the first place, clarify your core business and your market niche. Qualify your customers to assure that your products and services fit their interests, then delight them. If an existing customer or client cannot be effectively served, chances are great that both your customer and your business will benefit from making a change. If you find it necessary to "fire" a client, assist the client with finding a provider that better meets its needs and interests. Be of service to your customer, even as you assist the customer in relocating to a "new home" with a competitor. In the long run, you will discover that being selective about your customers is good business!

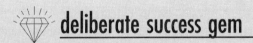 **deliberate success gem**

Managing by Values:
Becoming a Fortunate 500 Organization

Contributed by Kenneth Blanchard, Ph.D. & Michael O'Connor, Ph.D.

John Naisbitt, author of Megatrends and coauthor of *Reinventing the Corporation*, shared his dream with us that "someday there will be a list of Fortunate 500 companies." Although a Fortune 500 company is defined by size and volume, a Fortunate 500 company would be defined not only by its profitability, but also by the quality of service available to its customers and the quality of life accessible to its employees. We were immediately intrigued by the idea. With Naisbitt's encouragement, we have continued to explore and develop the concept.

An organization that can find solid footing in all its key business relationships, when so many others are slipping and sliding around, is indeed a fortunate one. A relatively simple and truly strategic plan exists for achieving this: CEOs.

C   stands for Customers.
E   stands for Employees.
O   stands for Owners.
S   stands for Significant other groups.

A Fortunate 500 organization focuses on delighting customers. You want customers who brag about you and become part of your marketing force. You have to treat customers in such a way that they become raving fans of your service.

A Fortunate 500 company creates an outstanding quality of life for its employees. Such a company creates a motivating environment for its people, one in which the employees can see that working toward the organization's goals is also in their mutual best interest. In this environment, employees think and act like owners. Employees are honored, empowered, and acknowledged.

A Fortunate 500 organization generates a profit for its owners or stockholders. This profit results from ethical activities that honor the fundamental principles and values of the company. A key point that distinguishes a Fortunate 500 organization from its competitors is the integrity of profit-making and the related resource allocation practices by management and its owners.

The fourth key of a Fortunate 500 organization is commitment to a mutually beneficial business relationship with significant other groups. These may be the community, creditors, suppliers, vendors, distributors, or even respected competitors. Building a win-win partnership relationship with these significant other groups enhances the quality of your products and services while building trusting business relationships. While enhancing the reputation of your industry and building customer confidence and loyalty, you are simultaneously positioning your firm for increased long-term profits.

A Fortunate 500 corporation has a vested interest in converting its mission and values into tangible results. This organization knows what it stands for and brings its management practices into alignment with this direction and philosophy. A Fortunate 500 company keeps employees committed, delights its customers, satisfies its stockholders, and creates a partnership environment with suppliers and creditors who are glad to be business associates. Managing by values can and does make a difference.

—Kenneth Blanchard, Ph.D.
Coauthor of *The One-Minute Manager* and
Managing By Values
www.blanchardlearning.com
—Michael O'Connor, Ph.D.
Coauthor of *The Platinum Rule* and
Managing By Values

What does your corporate culture demonstrate about customer service? To what extent are your teams committed to serving both the internal *and* external customers? To what extent are you empowering each person to bring out their best in service to others?

"Unless you have a trained, literate, motivated work force,
and give them decision-making authority,
you don't get satisfied customers."

—Anthony Rucci, Chief Administrative Officer, Sears

---

deliberate success
strategy 3: empowerment

releasing human potential

"I believe the real difference between
success and failure in a corporation
can very often be traced to the question
of how well the organization brings out
the great energies and talents of its people."

—Thomas J. Watson, Jr. Former IBM Chief Executive

chapter 7

empowerment:

tapping into your talent

"The highest reward for a man's work
is not what he gets for it,
but what he becomes by it."

—Hal Gooch
Quixtar Double Diamond

the high cost of disempowered, disengaged employees

"IT STOPPED BEING fun here 16 years ago," claimed a 42-year-old manager I interviewed in a new client organization. His numb spirit, glazed eyes, and low energy reflected both disengagement and disempowerment. His attitude, unfortunately, is not that uncommon in many corporate environments.

The March 13, 2001, issue of *The Wall Street Journal* reported that a study done by the Gallup Organization found that only 26 percent of workers were "engaged" in their work, 55 percent were "not engaged," and 19 percent of workers were "actively disengaged!" Workers complained that they don't know what is expected of them, they don't have the resources to do their jobs, they don't have a best friend at work, and they can't get the attention of their bosses.

The Gallup Organization estimates that this job disengagement costs anywhere from $292 billion to $355 billion a year. When 74 percent of employees are either "not engaged" or "actively disengaged," leaders in Corporate America need to pay careful attention to this wake-up call! Ignoring The Human Element—the "soft factors"—has a profoundly negative impact on The Bottom Line. It doesn't have to be that way.

"Are your skills, knowledge, and experience fully and effectively utilized on the job?" I frequently ask this question in leadership-development sessions. The responses are distressing. In most organizations, less than 5 percent respond affirmatively. Although admittedly an unscientific data collection process, this question focuses on a growing dilemma in Corporate America. Imagine the cost of lost human potential when a corporation fails to effectively engage a large portion of its workforce. Consider the effect on productivity, the loss of creative ideas, the impact on quality, and what this condition does to your competitive edge.

Consider the attitude of employees whose talents are underutilized and those who are "actively disengaged" from their work. How do you suppose they feel about themselves, about the work they produce, and about their employer? Disempowered, underutilized employees produce work that reflects these conditions. Employees don't like this kind of working environment, and business cannot afford this ineffective use of human capital. The only beneficiaries for failing to empower your employees are your competitors!

Empowerment is not a fad, not a program, not a technique. Empowerment is a way of being and doing to support, release, and encourage the effective use of individual and team talent while serving a shared organizational mission and vision. In the collaborative relationship between management and employees, an appropriate balance of authority and influence evolves in the pursuit of sustaining a competitive edge.

Jack Welsh, General Electric's recently retired chairman and CEO, believes that actively connecting with the heart and minds of people is critical for success in this competitive market. "I think any company," according to Welsh, "has got to find a way to engage the mind of every single employee. If you're not thinking all the time about making every person more valuable, you don't have a chance. What's the alternative? Wasted minds? Uninvolved people? A labor force that is angry or bored? That doesn't make sense!"[16]

Some unenlightened managers dismiss empowerment as just another buzzword or fad that will quickly be replaced by the next great management theory or program. Interestingly enough, empowerment has been around for a long, long time—and will continue to stay around in peak-performing organizations. More than 2,000 years ago, the Romans and Greeks utilized a form of empowered teams to stimulate creativity and support higher productivity.

Stockholders, board members, and corporate executives closely monitor return on investment (ROI). Monthly reports, quarterly reports, and annual reports focus on ROI and other financial indicators to assure that business investments generate a profitable return. Board meetings often concentrate on methods of reducing costs, increasing productivity, and increasing profits. Although financial trends are carefully explored, effective utilization of human resources is often ignored. If we say people are important but measure and reward only tangible results, the message of what we truly value is clear.

Many executives are not even aware of their unawareness regarding the neglect of human capital. **First**, hiring practices often do not match the interests and talents of the individual with what is needed in a particular position. **Second**, organizations typically do not provide sufficient coaching and development of staff to assure their long-term competence and confidence. And **third**, talents of people are frequently contained and underutilized by overly directive and controlling bosses. As a result, disempowered and underutilized employees tend to shoot for performance minimums. This loss of unrealized potential, passion, and productivity rarely registers on the corporate radar screen. Yet, the poor ROI on human capital could well be one of the most costly of all financial losses to American businesses. Examine your own business. What specifically are you doing that may diminish human talent and what are you doing to develop and release human talent?

Leaders and followers need each other, yet the struggle between authority and influence remains a difficult challenge. Warren Bennis, a seasoned leadership consultant, claims that employees are frequently "overmanaged and underled." Inconsistent leadership, on the other hand, results in switching back and forth between being too authoritarian and too permissive. Thomas Gordon, in his exploration of parent effectiveness, claims that "parents are authoritarian until they can't stand themselves and then permissive until they can't stand the kids." Managers, like parents, sometimes experience the same search for appropriate balance between having too much or too little control.

Within the next decade or two, predict Scott and Jaffe, the major sources of competitive advantage will lie not in new technology, but in the dedication, the quality of the commitment, and the competency of your workforce. The results of employee energy and creativity—human capital—are the company's most important resource.[17] Although developing and effectively utilizing technology is a major factor in sustaining your competitive edge, an element with even more impact in the next decade will be releasing untapped human potential. In most organizations, learning how to effectively empower others will ultimately have a more favorable impact on The Bottom Line than efforts to contain costs and enhance technology.

As the old authoritarian management model diminishes in effectiveness, leaders are gaining appreciation of the value of influence over authority and of empowerment over control. Influencing with integrity remains a far more powerful force than attempting to control and contain others. The late president Richard Nixon attempted to gather as much power and control as he could while in office. When matters started to slip out of control, he reacted by tightening his grip and maneuvering the political machinery to reestablish power. Strangely enough, the more he attempted to gain control, the less control he experienced. His behaviors demonstrated the paradox: The more one seeks to gain power, the less power he attains; the more one gives power away (empowers others), the more power and influence he receives.

As a former hospital administrator, I had a fair amount of "position power." Looking back, I had less influence, especially with certain physicians, than I care to admit. Now, as a leadership and organization-development consultant, I have zero authority in my client organizations. I don't have enough authority to even call a meeting! I generally have significant influence, however, in working with others to shape their corporate culture, develop leaders and teams, and achieve pragmatic results on priority issues.

The ability to influence rather than control creates a respectful environment, honors the differences and talents of people, releases human potential, and increases ownership of solutions. When all is said and done, people become advocates rather than adversaries of the corporate direction—even in their "parking lot" discussions. I would much rather have influence than authority.

Overzealous managers who seek to control the organization's environments stifle creativity and dampen enthusiasm. People operate out of fear or compliance rather than out of commitment. In his research article titled "Beyond Management to Leadership," John Keyser reported that "employees are most productive when they work within broadly-defined parameters, set their own objectives, direct their own work, and control their work environments."[18] The contemporary leader releases human potential, nurtures talents, supports creativity, coaches for mastery-level performance, and empowers associates to bring out their best in service to the organization.

Global competition, the pace of technological advancements, and rising customer expectations require employees who are entrusted to make decisions and resolve issues—often on the spot. A prerequisite of peak-performing organizations includes employees who can take initiative in addressing issues, who see the big picture, and who are accountable for results. That's the formula for success.

"Listening is a magnetic and strange thing, a creative force.
The friends who listen to us are the ones we move toward,
and we want to sit in their radius. When we are listened to, it creates us,
makes us unfold and expand."

—Karl Menninger

---

the deliberate success empowerment formula: E=f(M+A+C) x S

Empowerment gains the greatest momentum and achieves the most significant long-term results when individuals throughout the organization are inspired by a clearly defined mission and vision. Those working on the Apollo mission to the moon achieved a 40- to 50-percent sustained increase in performance because of the clarity of direction, unity of purpose, and passion associated with their history-making work. One does not, however, require such a lofty mission to inspire people. Associates at Les Schwab Tire Service in the Pacific Northwest are energized and passionate about their work—and they sell tires, for heaven's sake! Whether for the Apollo mission or at Les Schwab, the leaders understand the benefit of linking purpose, passion, and performance.

To achieve great results, employees must be provided with the essential tools to do the job—including the authority to act responsibly. How many times have you heard people say, "I have the responsibility but not the authority to do my job?" In many of those situations, however, they actually do have the authority but lack the courage to act. Whether it's lack of courage or lack of authority, this situation requires attention.

Recall a time when you wrote a check for groceries at your local market. Your check stopped the cashier cold in his tracks. He could go no further until first calling the manager over. Without looking at you or even asking any questions, the manager scribbled her initials on your check and immediately left for her next important task. At that point, who knows more about you: the cashier or the manager? At least the cashier has spent some time with you while ringing up your groceries. Who seems best qualified to make the judgment about approving the check? My vote goes to the cashier. What purpose, then, does the manager's approval serve? It's not what you think. It's not accountability and it's certainly not about adding value. It's job security for the manager; she needs something "important" to do! Management controls such as these disempower people and devalue their judgment.

In contrast, staff members I interviewed at the Salish Lodge near Seattle reported that they are empowered to call meetings with other departments, address problems, and implement solutions—all without the involvement of department directors. At the Ritz Carlton Hotels, housekeepers on each floor have the authority to make expenditures up to $2,000 to address customer needs. Employees are trusted to make quality decisions, and they act as though they own the place. In a vast majority of cases, competent employees who are trusted to make wise decisions honor that trust. Are you prepared to trust at that level?

Make it easier for your associates to use their talents. Link authority levels to the competence and experience of each employee. Push yourself to assure that the highest level of authority is provided to match the needs of the situation. A simple system of determining authority levels requires talking through which responsibilities they can carry out by: deciding on their own; deciding, then informing you and appropriate others about actions taken; or consulting first with you before acting.

During my former career in hospital administration, one of the department directors experienced frustration with my decision-making style and his lack of authority. Although I am a quick decision-maker, I was not quick enough for him. Sometimes I took three days to get back to him with a response to a proposal—far too long a wait for him. As a competent, action-oriented executive, he came up with a creative solution. The next proposal he sent in for my approval included a note that read: "Unless I hear differently from you, I intend to implement this plan in two days!" And he did! I had a superstar on my hands, and I needed to learn how to get out of his way and how to support making the best use of his talent.

"Much of what we call management simply gets in the way!"

—Peter Drucker

Creating an empowered environment still requires more than just commitment to mission and authority to make decisions. We need assurance that employees at all levels are competent to perform and that we have sufficient checks and balances in place. There are no shortcuts in identifying, developing, and sustaining competence. You have to be relentless in your commitment to both hiring and developing a competent staff. Building competence can best be achieved through an ongoing coaching process that will be fully explored in Deliberate Success Strategy 4 (Chapters 10–12) of this book.

Empowering confident, competent people produces results that count. The Empowerment Formula draws attention to those fundamental elements that assist in sustaining long-term organizational results. Each component of empowerment, in and of itself, does not produce the results most organizations seek. The synergistic combination of these elements, however, results in the kind of passion and commitment achieved within peak-performing organizations. Consider the following Empowerment Formula for enhancing results, individual by individual:

$$E = f(M + A + C) \times S$$

empowerment is:

a function of $\begin{pmatrix} \text{Mission} + \\ \text{Authority} + \\ \text{Competence} \end{pmatrix}$ **X** Stewardship

---

"The best thing a leader can do for a Great Group is to allow its members to discover their own greatness."

—**Warren Bennis and Ward Biederman** in *Organizing Genius*

Having a commitment to mission, providing authority, and assuring competence are still not enough to create the favorable conditions for empowerment. The presence of these elements, multiplied by "stewardship," completes the catalytic force of empowerment that catapults individuals and teams into peak levels of performance. Stewardship addresses the question "Is what I am doing right now serving the best interests of my company?" and touches that place within each person that makes him want to be his best, do his best, and respect organizational resources as if they were his own.

At Les Schwab Tire Centers, the "Pride In Performance" signs are not just a marketing ploy for the benefit of customers. Associates feel a genuine sense of pride and commit to doing their best in service to their customers. Pilots at Southwest Airlines seek ways to safely conserve fuel in an effort to keep costs down. The cultures of these organizations encourage intrinsic accountability rather than force compliance to company policies through strict supervision. Imagine the overall results when empowered employees commit to serving your mission and functioning as stewards of the resources—even when their supervisors are not around. With your associates, practice $E = f(M+A+C) \times S$ to engage their spirit, to tap into their talents, and to encourage stellar performance in converting the mission into tangible results.

trusting people to make sound decisions

Empowerment provides opportunities for employees to exercise sound judgment while developing problem-solving skills in addressing issues calling for attention. "We believe in you," instilled in the minds of new hires at Southwest Airlines through the "You, Southwest, and Success" (YSS) program, demonstrates a strong corporate commitment to honoring employees and trusting them to make sound decisions. Empowering employees to follow "Rule #1" generates a similar spirit at Nordstrom. What is Nordstrom's "Rule #1?" "Use your good judgment in all situations. There will be no additional rules."

If we talk empowerment yet continue to contain the talents of people through restrictive policies and practices, employees will quickly see through the smoke and mirrors. Employee frustration will increase as management credibility declines. If we are serious about empowerment, we need to align what we say with what we do. Many organizations, according to Stephen Covey, focus on failure avoidance rather than success enhancement. Doing both supports empowerment.

While conducting a 1:1 coaching session with the president of a 2,500-employee firm, an urgent knock came from the other side of his mahogany office door. One of his vice presidents poked his head in and asked if he had a minute. The president motioned him in and the vice president quickly described an urgent situation requiring attention.

The president listened and then said, "This is what I want you to do." He proceeded to give the vice president a step-by-step solution to the problem. When finished, he asked, "Any questions?" Having clear marching orders, the vice president had no questions and quickly left to handle the situation according to the wishes of the president.

After the vice president left, the president folded his arms, looked me square in my eyes, and asked, "Well, how did I do?" Consistent with my philosophy that the answers, most of the time, are within, I did not tell him how he did. I simply asked, "What did you teach him?" He paused for a moment, looked up at the ceiling, then said, "I blew it."

The president did "blow it," but he experienced important learning as we debriefed the situation. His pattern of taking learning opportunities away from others disempowered his entire executive team. In this coaching moment, the president came to the realization that he taught his vice president to seek him out when he had a problem, to let someone else to the thinking, and to shift accountability upward in the organization. When reflecting on his style further, he became aware that he handled most situations in a similar manner. It was no wonder the company experienced a lack of progress. His behavior demonstrated a fundamental lack of trust in his associates. When managers contain rather than release talent, associates experience a decline of fulfillment of The Human Element—and The Bottom Line ultimately suffers.

"Instead of giving them an order, ask: '
What would it take to be able to do this yourself?
Let's work together to have that happen.'
This infuses you with authentic power
rather than external power."

—Wayne Dyer

It takes courage for managers to turn decisions over to their associates, especially in difficult situations. It takes courage to clarify outcomes and empower people to figure out ways to fulfill those expectations. In many ways, it is a misuse of authority to solve problems that rightfully belong to people further out in the organization. If managers do not trust their associates to make appropriate decisions, or if managers are not utilizing the resources of associates, I have to ask why they keep them on the payroll.

Empowerment with accountability supports problem-solving closest to the problem's source. A challenge for leaders is to coach people to handle the issues within their competency levels and sphere of influence. Although coaching others to accept accountability requires time in the short run, the long-range return on investment is significant. The following experience demonstrates the principle:

A vice president in a large hospital approached me with a concern about the performance of a department director responsible to her. The vice president seemed stuck in this sensitive situation and wanted to explore how to effectively work through the issue.

I asked her to explain to me what the situation was and how she proposed to handle it. After talking through the proposed situation and action plan, I asked her to tell me about the advantages and disadvantages of that particular approach. She thoughtfully addressed the pros and cons, and then asked me, "What do you think?"

Upon hearing my favorable response, she smiled, got up from the conference table, and started to leave. I asked, "Where are you going?" Looking a bit puzzled, she said, "I thought you liked my approach." "What you shared with me was a great option. Now sit down and give me another great option! This time, I encouraged, "approach the issue from a different perspective. Stretch your creativity to generate yet another sound solution."

A bit frustrated with me, she started all over again from a different perspective. Her new solution, although quite different, had considerable merit. I asked her once again to identify the advantages and disadvantages of her second approach. After talking through the second approach, she asked, "What do you think?" I said, "I like the approach; you thought it through well." "Do you like it better than the first?" she quizzed. Hearing my favorable response, she once again started to leave.

"Where are you going?" I asked. "You're kidding!" she responded. "No. Now sit down and give me a third great answer," I told her. Once again she worked through the process of approaching the situation differently, then

exploring the advantages and disadvantages. I asked her to compare options one, two, and three and then to se- lect one that would best serve the long-term interests of both the organization and the individual involved. Al- though each option would have resolved the situation, she selected option three as the most effective.

The vice president thinks I am a great consultant! What did I do? Not much—other than to challenge her to tap into her own resources, to encourage her to create options, and to hold her accountable in resolving her own issues. By challenging her to search for the "third great answer," she not only owned the solution, but she is better prepared to draw upon her internal talents the next time a problem confronts her. She experienced the benefit of link- ing empowerment with accountability. And she experienced the benefit of looking for the "third great answer!"

I simply guided her through her own thought process of dis- covering that which she already knew. At least 80 percent of the time, according to my experience in coaching individuals, the answers are within. As a leader, challenge yourself to draw the answers out—not to put them in. Communicate your high ex- pectations of others and express confidence in their abilities. Use immediate situations as coaching opportunities to encour- age others to apply their talents. The following questions and observations assist in accomplishing those outcomes:

- How do you plan to handle that situation?
- What do you see as the "third-great answer" in deal- ing with that issue?
- How will the company be better off in the long run by following your recommendation?
- I have confidence in your ability to come up with a solution that will meet your needs and the company

interests at the same time. I'm counting on you to develop a creative solution.

- My job is to *assist* you in solving the problem; I'm not here to solve your problems *for you*.
- What do you see as the advantages and disadvantages of that approach?
- All I am expecting of you is to give your best. Is this your best shot?

"People become really quite remarkable
when they start thinking that they can do things.
When they believe in themselves,
they have the first secret of success."

—Norman Vincent Peale

"Is this empowerment thing for real or just empty words?" challenged Loren Ankarlo, a consultant specializing in self-directed work teams. In an executive seminar I attended, Ankarlo challenged us to go beyond "phantom empowerment." To test the progress of empowerment in your organization, ask:

1. What can you do today that you could not do six months ago?
2. Without the approval of your boss, can you:
   - Spend money?
   - Order supplies?
   - Order equipment?
   - Talk with his or her boss?
   - Initiate quality enhancements?
   - Call an interdepartmental meeting?
   - Stop the production line?

Employees who have demonstrated competence and steward-ship need to be empowered to use their talents most effectively in service to the organization. Are you on track with regard to building their competence and releasing their talents? Are you sufficiently balancing their personal and professional fulfillment with meeting the needs of your company?

linking empowerment with accountability

"When individuals are not trusting and trustworthy, empowerment does not work. Control is necessary."

—Stephen Covey

To mutually benefit the organization and the individual, em-powerment needs to implemented in the context of account-ability, partnership, and stewardship. Unrestrained empower-ment can lead to catastrophic results, as the following experi-ence demonstrates:

The managers of Baring's Bank of England appar-ently forgot to link empowerment with accountability in their zeal to expand decision-making authority. Twenty-eight-year-old Nicholas Leeson, manager of futures trad-ing in Singapore, unilaterally invested the bank's re-sources in the Japanese stock market. The investment turned sour. Having lost a significant amount, he at-tempted to gain the money back by investing even more, anticipating that the Japanese Nikkei index would rise. Only a few days later, however, the 1995 Kobe earth-quake caused the Nikkei index to plummet. The next morning, Baring's Bank woke up to losses of more than $1.3 billion, putting the 200-year-old bank out of busi-ness and causing the loss of more than 4,000 jobs.[19]

Empowerment without accountability comes with high risk.

Empowering employees requires an accountability contract—something that Baring's Bank discovered far too late. In exchange for a stronger voice in decision-making, empowered employees need to provide a greater commitment to serving the needs of the entire organization, a fair exchange for their enhanced role.[20] With empowerment comes responsibility and commitment, and it cannot be any other way.

W.L. Gore and Associates, the maker of Gor-Tex, employs a practice of empowering others within the context of what it refers to as the "waterline" check. Mistakes made above the waterline will not sink the ship. Mistakes below the waterline could well jeopardize the entire business. Those about to embark on high-risk ventures (below the waterline) are expected to carefully consult with all others within the company who might be affected.[21] This commitment to empowerment within the context of serving the larger interest of the company has proven to be a highly profitable practice for W.L. Gore and Associates while contributing to a more personally fulfilling work environment.

Empowerment with accountability requires being a good steward of the company resources and giving your best in service to the organization. Sometimes people resist accepting responsibility, as the following experience demonstrates:

> *When interviewing a group of executives prior to a scheduled planning and team-development workshop, several executives complained that empowerment had gone too far; they were trusted with making decisions beyond their comfort zone. At times, they needed an opportunity just to talk with the president and use him as a "sounding board" in the development of ideas.*

deliberate success gem

Empowerment: Freedom In Exchange For A Promise

Contributed by Peter Block, Ph.D.

Empowerment comes with a price. In exchange for receiving a stronger voice in decision-making, partners need to commit to act in the best interests of the whole organization. Freedom and commitment are, in every case, joined at the hip.

This commitment or promise is the key hedge against employee anarchy and entitlement. We give choice and flexibility to our associates, and in turn we exact a promise of certain outcomes. That means the place has to work and deliver results. The boss has a right and obligation to determine boundaries and define financial, productivity, quality, and client outcomes.

Membership in an organization means we have chosen and accepted this playing field. This choice and acceptance becomes our contract. Our desires for compensation, self-expression, and participation are viable only so long as we can commit to the mission, results, constraints, principles, and goals of the larger organization.

If our associates cannot commit to this contract, they should leave or we should fire **(cont.)**

In exploring that issue with the president, he provided an interesting insight about those who consistently sought him out as a "sounding board." "The real issue," he observed, "is not my availability as a sounding board. I am always available for that purpose. The real issue is their lack of courage to address issues. Some of the executives want to engage me in a discussion merely to cover their tails. If they talk to me first and make a decision that does not turn out well, they find it easy to say, 'Remember I talked with you already about that?' I want executives who can stand on their own and make the tough decisions they need to make without using me as a crutch—or to later blame me if it doesn't *work out well." Empowerment requires courage and accountability. Some find it difficult to accept that level of responsibility.*

"Liberty means responsibility. That is why most men dread it."

—George Bernard Shaw

At Clackamas Community College (CCC), near Portland, Oregon, employee participation is deeply embedded into the culture. In an interview with CCC President John Keyser prior to his retirement, he emphasized that "the college strives to maintain an open and inclusive organizational structure that enables all members of staff to participate in the

(**cont. from p. 140**) them, even if it takes three lawyers and three years. Agreement on the elements of the stewardship contract is the foundation for partnership and the basis for community. Stewardship offers more choice and local control in exchange for a firm commitment. This promise to serve the larger organization requires clarity right at the beginning.

Confronting self-serving and irresponsible actions becomes a tough challenge. A certain percentage of people will abuse their freedom, take advantage of a loose structure, or be disruptive with their peers. In the spirit of participation, managers sometimes pull back too far. When confronting dysfunctional behavior, we get accused of being insincere in our efforts to empower others. We are told we are not walking our talk. Don't buy it! There is tyranny in the claim that we cannot confront people or even express anger when we are partners. The fact that some will abuse empowerment does not signal the return to dictatorial management. We are just going ask certain individuals or teams to perform consistent with their promise to function in the best interests of the company in exchange for their enhanced role. With freedom comes responsibility—and that cannot be neglected.

—Peter Block, Ph.D.
Author of *Stewardship* and *The Empowered Manager*
www.peterblock.com

decision-making process." Every staff member is connected to the information-sharing and decision-making network at several levels, beginning at the departmental work group and extending to a variety of committees and councils. The intent is to seek the widest possible input to address broad issues, to provide a diversity of communications, and to assure inclusion of both staff and community. In exchange for this increased level of involvement, "all college personnel must contribute to and support the educational mission of the college."

A core value at CCC, according to Keyser, is the belief that "every staff member is a problem solver, with the right and responsibility to identify and resolve issues they encounter on the job." Staff members are encouraged to ask themselves how they can improve service to students, respond to emerging needs, take advantage of new opportunities, operate more efficiently, and create a better future for CCC.

W.L. Gore and Associates, Clackamas Community College, 3M, Merck, Johnson & Johnson, and other such organizations demonstrate the value of empowerment, not just by policy, but through their behaviors. They provide people with latitude and freedom, yet expect high levels of performance in return.

"Life does not happen to you; it happens from you."

—Mike Wickett

Accountability starts with you. Whether in your personal life or in your business environment, learning to take responsibility for the results you create, both the successes and failures, is the foundation of personal and professional excellence.

fostering empowerment through artful delegation

Effective leaders clearly understand the power and psychology of artful delegation as an effective empowerment tool. Two types of delegation occur: delegating to "strength" and delegating to "stretch." When delegating to "strength," the individual has already demonstrated competence. Management can count on that person being knowledgeable, completing the project with quality and accuracy, and getting the project done quickly.

Consistently delegating similar projects to the same, qualified person, however, may deprive others from learning and even repeat mediocre habits. Additionally, what if your favorite expert gets hit by a Mack truck or leaves the organization for a better job? If backup talent has not been developed, you get the opportunity to deal with an immediate productivity crisis.

Delegating to "stretch," however, provides a different set of disadvantages and advantages. In this case, the individual does not know how to do the assignment. Delegating to "stretch" comes with a number of disadvantages: Count on consuming more time and resources, making errors, experiencing initial quality discrepancies, and possibly even negatively impacting customer service. On the other hand, engaging new people in assignments can stimulate their interest, infuse new creative ideas, and develop a broader base of expertise to provide qualified backup.

When delegating, determine in advance which strategy ("strength" or "stretch") will produce the best overall results. If you have hired well and they have the talent, trust your associates to do the right thing as you raise the bar. Expect the best and coach them to achieve Deliberate Success.

The late Admiral Grace Hopper, near the close of her brilliant career in the U.S. Navy, worked with young officers to teach them how to use their talent effectively and to circumvent the Navy bureaucracy when necessary. She encouraged the budding officers to trust themselves to do the right thing, to demonstrate courage in dealing with issues calling for attention, and to take action. Admiral Hopper coined the phrase: "It is easier to ask for forgiveness than to ask for permission."

Give your associates as much authority as they can handle, and then stretch them even further. Work with your associates and encourage them to apply their unique knowledge and skills. Stand behind them when they make a mistake, and look for the learning rather than the culprit. If you have hired and developed competent, accountable people, trust them to sound decisions, and get out of their way. Empowered, engaged, enthusiastic people simply perform well.

"If we all did the things we are capable of doing, we would literally astound ourselves."

—Thomas Alva Edison

chapter 8

unity, not uniformity

honoring differences and aligning talent

"Of all the things I've done, the most vital is coordinating the talents of those who work for us and pointing them toward a certain goal."

—**Walt Disney**

differences are resources

ALFRED SLOAN, THE celebrated first president of General Motors decades ago, struggled with a major policy issue. As the story goes, he called in his chief advisors to gain the advantage of their experience and counsel. At the conclusion of their deliberations, he asked each executive around the conference table where they stood on the issue. Solid support. In fact, the executives easily reached a unanimous decision. A majority vote, let alone unanimous support, would have delighted most presidents. Not Alfred Sloan.

When confronted with his top team being in unanimous agreement, Sloan delivered an unsettling message to them: "Because we are in unanimous agreement on this critical issue, I am tabling the decision. We cannot afford to have each of us of the same opinion. I am paying for your judgment, not for your agreement." (Editorial note: I took a few liberties in paraphrasing his message.) He tabled the decision and terminated the meeting. Some weeks later, they revisited the issue—and developed a more effective solution than the one unanimously supported.

What did Sloan teach them? That it is safe to disagree. That differences are valued and welcomed. That different perspectives enrich the decision-making process. That differences are resources.

An organization requires two seemingly opposing forces to perform and prosper: differentiation and integration. Just as different body organs provide essential functions to sustain the human biological system, different organizational functions and talents are required to create and sustain organizational excellence.

Effective leaders commit to honoring and empowering differences while aligning talent to support a shared direction—equivalent to "getting your wild geese to fly in formation."[22] The differing talents of people equates to the "wild geese"; serving a shared mission and vision equates to "flying in formation." Working together, these differing elements unite to produce great results.

Getting everyone in line, similar to the behavior of Sloan's executive team, compares with "getting your ducks in a row." Alfred Sloan made it clear to his team that he wanted "wild geese" on the team, not a bunch of ducks lining up in agreement. When two business partners always agree, one of them is unnecessary.

integrating differences

The message is clear. You want *unity* of spirit and direction, not *uniformity*. Unity builds synergy and commitment and honors the differences required to produce effective results. Uniformity breeds apathy and resentment and diminishes the collective talents of individuals and teams.

Each person has a unique set of talents that, when effectively integrated into the culture, can make a significant contribution. Sometimes, however, we look upon the differences of others as deficiencies or detractors. Suppose, for example, you are a member of an organizational team that has a vacant position. When seeking to fill this position, you typically look for similarities (individuals who agree with your philosophy) and differences (individuals who complement your team through their unique experiences and training).

Intrigued with the potential of hiring a person with new ideas and a fresh perspective, you find the "perfect" combination of similarities and differences within a single candidate. The person has a brilliant history of contributing at her past places of employment and is credited with generating numerous useful ideas. With enthusiasm, you introduce this experienced person to your team. At the first team meeting, she enthusiastically shares several ideas that worked particularly well in her former place of employment.

Upon hearing her ideas, team members glance at one another in silence. Then excuses start flowing: *"We tried that before, and it didn't work." "In this organization, we do it this way." "The boss will never buy it." "You haven't been here long enough to understand our unique situation." "It's not in the budget."* Although somewhat exaggerated, this resistive behavior seems to be far too common in many organizations. We intentionally hire a "square peg" then try to stuff it in a round hole with the rest of us. We talk unity, then practice uniformity. In most corporate cultures, it doesn't take too long to knock off the corners of a new hire—and to make him or her just like the rest of us.

Some years ago, I consulted with a city government as it began its transition from an authoritarian to an empowering organizational culture. Both management and employees demonstrated intrigue with the emerging direction, yet struggled with "old baggage" from the past that made it difficult to move off of their position. In one of a series of three-day cultural change workshops I facilitated, the president of the firefighters union strongly reacted to this new "empowerment crap." He had plenty of evidence that management "couldn't care less about empowerment," as his following story reveals:

"Ever since I was a boy, I wanted to be a fire fighter. After graduating from the fire academy, I was hired by this city. My proudest moment occurred 10 years ago when I walked into the fire station wearing my new uniform, cap, and badge. This was a dream come true.

Instead of welcoming me to the station, the captain came up to me, took my cap off, and threw it on the floor! He then jammed a McDonalds's hamburger hat over my ears and ordered me to clean the latrine. The rest of the more senior fire fighters mocked me as I cleaned toilets while wearing my hamburger hat."

In the first 10 minutes of employment, the captain killed his spirit. During his "orientation" period (some would call it "hazing"), he learned that the fire department had two teams: "us" and "them." Ten years later, the now more experienced firefighter still works for the same captain. Yet, things are different. That firefighter now presides over a very militant union. And it's payback time. Efforts to improve the situation are now significantly hampered by unresolved situations from the past. If you do not deal with significant issues of the past, the past will catch up and deal with you.

Getting your "wild geese to fly in formation" is challenging enough without past history that may be in the way. Yet, if we "camp out" in our history, necessary changes will never occur. Although everyone will not necessarily join you in your efforts to create a more empowering culture, most will welcome the opportunity. You may not be able to make a new start with some, but you can work together in creating a new ending.

Building alignment between the interests of the employees and the interests of the organization can be a powerful force. Look for every opportunity to "create giants" of others as you consciously shape your culture, as my experience at Southwest Airlines demonstrates:

> *As a passenger on Southwest Airlines last year, I encountered another way of integrating a new employee onto the staff. The senior flight attendant playfully commanded our attention over the public address system, "Attention ladies and gentlemen, boys and girls. I have the honor of introducing to you Shirley, our newest flight attendant to join our team. Southwest hires the best of the best, and Shirley exceeded every one of our high standards. In fact, she is soooo good that she can handle the toughest of problems that you give to her! Even though this is her very first flight, those of you who have really tough issues, please direct them to Shirley." At that point, everyone laughed and spontaneously erupted into a welcome applause for Shirley. Her wide grin said a lot.*

Compare the new firefighter's first day with Shirley's first day. Notice how quickly cultural differences impacts attitude and performance. Examine how new employees are treated in your own organization. Are they assigned to the poorest shifts and given the "grunt" work that other people don't want? Are they quickly demotivated or are they energized? Those first few days and weeks often shape attitudes that last for the rest of an employee's association with an organization.

What attitudes are you creating in those early days of employment in your organization? What are new employees saying to their associates about their job? What are they saying to their spouse at home about their new job? What would you like them to be saying? Are you prepared to make the revolutionary changes required in your culture?

Honoring differences provides latitude for employees to use their talents at the highest level. Instead of chipping off their corners, celebrate their differences. We need the *wild geese,* yet we need them to *fly in formation.* Bringing out the best of others while aligning talent in service to the organization requires building a spirit of unity, creating a passion for the possible, and holding ourselves and others accountable to create desired results. Make winners out of your current associates, and make sure you hire only winners as you transform your organization.

"Nothing happens unless you have a personal transformation."

—W. Edwards Deming

chapter 9

the "3 a's" of hiring winners:

attitude, aptitude, and alignment

*"You can buy a pretty good dog,
but you can't buy his tail wagging."*

—Thornton Wilder

CAN YOU THINK of a person who should never have been hired into a particular job? Have *you* ever hired the wrong person for a position? When a person is poorly suited for a job, that individual, the organization, and its customers all seem to be adversely affected. Think also about the time and resources an inappropriately placed person consumes and how those same resources could have been used to instead grow and develop your competent employees.

Before you can empower others with confidence, you need to make sure you have the right people in the right jobs. And that starts with making one of the most important decisions you can make: hiring winners. When hiring, consider three non-negotiable criteria to assure long-term success: attitude, aptitude, and alignment.

attitude

the 3 "a's"
of
hiring winners

aptitude

alignment

the right attitude

Hiring people with the "right" *attitude* about work ethics, customer service, teamwork, and quality performance will position you immediately to achieve significant and positive results. Hiring winners enables you to start off at a high level of performance and raise the bar from there. Conversely, *"hiring in haste provides the opportunity,"* according to Brian Tracy, *"to repent in leisure."* You know how costly it is to retain the wrong person. Never "settle" for in the hiring process—go for gold.

An executive I interviewed at Nordstrom reported, "We are more interested in how candidates fit into the Nordstrom culture and their commitment to customer service than we are in what is on their resume." A Maytag executive made a similar comment to me. Southwest Airlines "hires for attitude and trains for skill." Stephen Jobs, cofounder of Apple Computers, reported: "We hire really great people and create an environment where people can make mistakes and grow."

Hewitt Associates, a peak-performing compensation- and benefits-consulting firm, does one of the best jobs I have seen in hiring and developing winners. In the decade that I consulted with Hewitt, I consistently experienced talented people who were encouraged to use their knowledge and skills in service to their clients. Note what their chief executive has to share in the following "Deliberate Success Gem" about hiring "SWANs."

Success-oriented organizations hire well, then coach and empower these talented people to develop their full potential. Don't be seduced into hiring even a highly skilled applicant whose attitude raises yellow flags. In the long run, your business and your customers will be far better off in hiring an individual having both a positive attitude and a stellar aptitude to do the job, even though her skills might not yet be fully developed. Her skills can be taught through a systematic coaching

 deliberate success gem

Leading In a High-Performance Culture

Contributed by Dale Gifford

The culture of an organization can have a powerful impact on the success of the enterprise and its employees. This impact is especially positive when it's aligned with the attitudes and natural inclinations of employees. As a consulting firm, we see this phenomenon at work in our clients, and we've applied this with a strong result in our own business.

A first element of culture is to develop the key motivating goal or goals of the enterprise. While some people might be strongly motivated by a mantra such as "maximizing shareholder value," most people I know don't fall into that category. Hewitt Associates has always expressed a more complex, but also more motivating triad of goals:

1. Exceptional service to our clients.
2. A satisfying work experience for our associates.
3. Financial success for the business.

In a more typical publicly held consumer business, this could be summarized as a simultaneous passion for customers, employees, and shareholders.

The second element is creating or reinforcing principles for how people work together **(cont.)**

(cont. from p. 153) and treat each other in the process. Because teamwork and quick responsiveness to client needs are critical success factors in our business, our principles focus on such items as open communication, respect, personal growth and accountability, avoidance of profit centers, minimization of status trappings, and so forth.

The third, and in many ways the most important, element is hiring and promoting individuals based not only on their skills, but also on the consistency of their attitudes and personal characteristics with these cultural imperatives. Although it lengthens and complicates the screening process, it results in greater commitment, long-term reinforcement of the culture, and much lower turnover. A simple acronym (SWAN) we've often used as a shorthand tool for evaluating candidates summarizes these key characteristics for us:

S: Smart

W: Works hard and smart

A³: Ambitious (driven, but not competitive with others internally), Adaptable, Accountable

N: Nice (appreciated by our clients and consistent with our second goal of a "satisfying work experience")

Alignment among the organization's key goals, people principles, and hiring and promoting criteria produces a powerful and high performance culture.

—Dale Gifford
Chief Executive, Hewitt Associates
www.was.hewitt.com/hewitt/

and training process. You say you can't afford to take the time to train someone for the job? Consider the time and expense you will ultimately experience if your hire the wrong person. Attitude counts—and counts big.

the right aptitude

If you need an eagle, hire an eagle—not a duck. Ducks cannot be turned into eagles no matter what you do. A person has to have the *aptitude* to perform the job effectively. Even with a positive attitude, an inept person without the ability to attain a high skill level in the desired area will not perform effectively. Even a happy, well-adjusted, positive duck cannot soar with the eagles. Make sure those you hire have the core talent to perform the job requirements with mastery.

Professional coaches do a particularly good job of finding talented athletes. The coaches don't take chances. They send their talent scouts out to observe the players in action. Coaches look for three key deliverables:

1. Does the athlete demonstrate the core talent to do the job well?
2. Is the athlete a team player?
3. Will the athlete bring added value to the team?

The athlete must excel in all three to qualify for consideration. Anything less than a high grade is not acceptable.

To what extent have you developed your skills as a "talent scout?" Are you seeking out and finding the best of the best, or are you letting a mediocre hiring process attract mediocre talent? What consequences might you pay for hiring and then empowering poor to mediocre performing employees?

the right alignment

Alignment, the third non-negotiable hiring criteria, addresses the necessity of assuring a match between the individual and organizational mission, vision, and values. When these elements align, you can tap into the passion of people to create and sustain even long-term performance results.

Disney loads the process for success by requiring every employee to attend an extensive orientation taught by the faculty of Disney University. This thoughtfully planned program aligns each new employee with the traditions, culture, and Disney way of doing business. New employees experience a sense of belonging to a special team that creates magic in the lives of their theme park guests. Even the Disney annual reports to stockholders emphasize such terms as *dreams, fun, joy, imagination,* and *magic.* [23]

> *"The question isn't: 'What if we train people and they leave?'*
> *The question should be: 'What if we don't train people and they stay?'"*
>
> **—Brian Tracy**

A spirit of partnership is achieved when leaders link individual vision and values with organizational vision and values. The greater the alignment between individual and organizational vision and values, the higher the commitment. The farther individual and organizational vision and values are apart, the greater the resistance. Pay attention when you experience resistance from others; they are trying to tell you something!

Establishing a spirit of partnership at the time of hire greatly facilitates nurturing that relationship throughout the employee's tenure with your company. Where do you see most of your employees being on the following partnership scale, ranging from "Active Resistance" to "Commitment"? What costs might you experience if they are at the lower end of the scale, and what benefits accrue from employees positioned at the top of the scale? Although you cannot legislate or mandate commitment, you can certainly create an environment in which people choose to be committed and choose to give their very best.

> *"If people don't have their own vision,*
> *all they can do is 'sign up' for someone else's.*
> *The result is compliance, never commitment."*
>
> **—Peter Senge**

Linking each person to the mission becomes a powerful resource in releasing talent, building a spirit of partnership, and empowering associates to achieve impressive results. General managers of most Marriott Hotels make daily rounds to both listen to

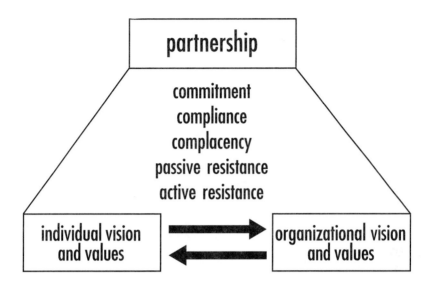

and talk with employees about how what they do today contributes to corporate objectives. The late Mary Kay Ash recognized and rewarded even small steps made by her "consultants" in their cosmetic business development—a win-win outcome that supported the corporate mission while benefiting individuals.

Empowerment cannot be just a platitude. It must have substance—practical application that converts the concept into reality. For empowerment to benefit the organization and the individuals, human potential must be released rather than contained. Start by hiring talented people. Empower them in the context of accountability to perform in service to the organization. Then commit to their continued development through ongoing coaching. By effectively engaging their spirit and passion, you create a win for them and a win for your organization.

"How does your work touch the joy in you,
and what joy does your work bring out in others?"

—**Matthew Fox**

---

deliberate success
strategy 4: coaching

creating giants of others

"The best managers start with a radical assumption:
Each person's greatest room for growth
is in the area of his greatest strength."

—Marcus Buckingham

chapter 10

performance coaching:

positioning others for success

> "The job of a wise teacher
> is to help another to become."
>
> —Stephen Covey

treasure-hunting: the role of an effective coach

HELEN KELLER SUFFERED an early childhood disease that left her blind and deaf. Locked into her dark, quiet inner world, she had no known way to connect with her outer world. As a bright child with no means to communicate, she became incorrigible.

Her parents did not know what to do with her. They ultimately hired a teacher named Annie Sullivan. Annie had a deep sense of compassion, for she too had been blind for part of her life and had dealt with abuse issues. Instead of asking, "What can I do with her?" Annie asked herself, "What can I do for her?"

Annie knew that this difficult child had hidden treasures locked up inside. As a "coach," Annie committed herself to finding a way to unlock those hidden talents. But first, she needed to invent a creative way to communicate with this deaf and blind child. Over and over, Annie signed words into the palm of Helen's hand. No connection. No understanding. No results.

On one occasion, however, while pouring water into Helen's hand and signing "w-a-t-e-r," the tangible object and the abstract word finally came together. Annie found the right combination! And the learning began.

Through the committed and tenacious efforts of a teacher who saw potential in the life of another, Annie opened the emotional and intellectual floodgates of one of the most remarkable people in recent history. Helen Keller later wrote of that magic moment, "The word dropped into my mind like the sun in a frozen winter world, and I woke up!"

Although Helen Keller was a giant of a person, imagine what her life would have been like without the powerful influence of Annie Sullivan. Annie committed herself to releasing the giant within Helen. Annie functioned as a coach to develop Helen Keller's talents. And Helen Keller went on to make major contributions to our world.

Treasure-hunting—developing others while achieving organizational results—is fundamental to peak-performing companies and represents the essence of the coaching process. Peak-performing organizations work at being excellent. They consciously seek to enhance productivity and profitability while bringing out the best in people. Leaders in search of Deliberate Success recognize and honor the intrinsic value of each person's contribution to the overall success of the organization. Employees respond by producing impressive results—and that's what counts.

Some managers have the mistaken belief that they have to know more or be more skilled than the employees they coach. Not necessarily so! Consider Olympic athletes. Each athlete has a coach, yet I am confident that none of the coaches can out-perform the athletes. Recall Kerri Strug, the 1996 gymnastic Olympian who secured the first U.S. team gold medal in women's gymnastic team history. Remember when she hurt her ankle upon completing her final event? Remember when her coach, Bela Karolyi, carried her up to the Gold Medal platform? Given his large size, I doubt that he could even do 10 chin-ups on the bar (sorry, Coach Karolyi!), but he coached Kerri to perform magically.

You don't have to know more than those you coach, and you don't even need to out-perform those you coach. It is important for you, however, to be a great coach. Winning coaches create winning teams. These same coaches have clarity of mission, seek out talented players to join the team, work with each athlete to develop his or her individual potential, and consciously seek to create a spirit of teamwork and synergy among the entire group. They do not leave success up to luck. These coaches are deliberately successful and consciously seek to build great teams that deliver impressive results. You can do the same.

turning people on about their jobs

I am often asked to give seminars and convention talks on "motivating others." This presents a dilemma for me, because I believe motivation comes from within the individual rather than from external forces. Additionally, my seminar on motivation lasts only 45 seconds and has only two points:

1. Find out what turns people on about their job and do *more* of that.
2. Find out what turns people off about their job and do *less* of that!

End of seminar on motivation.

Critics respond to this message with such statements as, "That seems so simplistic. Give me something more complicated!" The power of motivation is contained within the simplicity, not in the complexity. Think about it. If you genuinely explore what turns people on about their job and consciously seek to link their interests with the company needs, you can release a positive and powerful force. The leadership challenge switches from trying to kick people in the seat of the pants to get them to do something to periodically having to hold them back as their creativity and commitment soars.

Empowering others ignites the human spirit and releases purposeful creativity. Linking individual with organizational vision and values enables both the associates and the company to prosper in this exciting, productive environment.

Have you ever been asked by a manager, "What turns you on about your job, and what can I do to enable you to experience even greater job and career fulfillment?" In the many coaching seminars I have conducted for thousands of leaders, I frequently explore if any of those present have ever been asked a question like that. Even though managing is often defined as "getting things done through people," less than 5 percent have *ever* been asked a question of this nature by their managers. Most cannot conceive of a boss being even remotely interested enough to ask such a question.

The fortunate few who have been asked this question by their boss report feeling valued, empowered, cared about, and important. How would you feel if your manager genuinely explored what you like about your job, listened attentively to your responses, then worked closely with you to create an even more satisfying and productive work environment? I bet your commitment to the company would escalate.

In describing their behaviors following this experience, people have consistently shared an increased sense of enthusiasm and elevated commitment to both the manager and the organization. Imagine an entire workforce that felt valued, empowered, cared about, and important! Imagine what happens to performance when you align purposes and while tapping into their passion.

Why do managers so often ignore asking this important question? They fear the response. They fear that the "wild goose" might not fly in formation. They think, *"What if they want my job? What if the associates ask for something that I cannot produce?"* Rather than open up Pandora's Box, some managers prefer to just ignore the issue altogether. Staying within the managerial comfort zone seems safer than risking possible change.

In contrast, confident leaders have the courage to explore what turns people on and off about their jobs. Enlightened leaders actively engage associates in the process of designing and shaping their jobs and work assignments to enhance fulfillment, to more effectively utilize their talents and interests, and to increase productivity. More often than not, associates give thoughtful responses to this question and seek responsible, accountable ways to create results that work for both them and for the organization.

Most everyone has a part of their job that they do not particularly enjoy. What if, however, you reassigned a responsibility from one who does not enjoy performing that particular function to one who finds that same work interesting or even challenging? Accommodating individual interests while serving organizational needs requires imagination and open communication. Engaging your associates in this job refinement process communicates that you care — and they tend to reciprocate.

Organization behavioral research consistently reports that the primary motivators of people are doing something that results in people feeling good about themselves and doing something worthwhile—in other words, making a difference. Compensation, on the other hand, occupies a much lower status on the list of motivators. (If one is unemployed or under employed, however, compensation has a higher priority.) Effective coaches tap into these internal motivators and structure work assignments such that both the individual and organization benefit.

"We cannot become who we need to be by remaining as we are."

—Max DePree

---

we "teach" others to perform poorly—really!

We teach others how to perform, either directly or indirectly, either intentionally or unintentionally. In fact, managers in many organizations teach employees to perform poorly by not clarifying direction and expectations, not coaching others to bring out their best, not reinforcing good performance, and not confronting poor performance. Employees learn that just going through the motions of showing up for work entitles them to a paycheck. Productivity and quality performance seem to take a subordinate position. Under these conditions, management promotes mediocrity—and then wonders why it lost its competitive edge to its competitors!

The March 2001 issue of *HR Magazine* reported on a study of executives conducted by Manchester Inc., of Jacksonville, Florida, in which participants estimated that coaching yielded a return of 5.7 times their initial investment. Seventy-seven percent agreed that coaching helped improve their working relationships with direct reports, 71 percent with immediate supervisors, and 63 percent with peers. Job satisfaction improved for 61 percent of respondents. Coaching provides a cost-effective method of reconnecting with employees and linking individual with organizational interests.

"You can have everything in life you want if you can help other people get what they want."

— Zig Zigler

Coaching provides a remarkably high ROI, yet many managers essentially ignore the potential value of this important resource. When managers do "coach," however, they often limit their efforts to those who have difficulties on the job. The best performers—those who, ironically, can benefit the most from coaching—are often ignored. Managers often erroneously believe that good performers don't need to be coached and thus put forth 80 percent of their efforts on the poorest performers. Who gets the most coaching attention in your organization: your best or your poorest performers?

Bring to mind a person who has either "retired on the job" or has demonstrated chronically poor performance. Perhaps you can think of several people. What happens to substandard performers? In many organizations, poor performers are ignored, passed over for promotion, or even transferred to another department—with "good" references, of course!

Under these circumstances, poor performers merely collect their paychecks without performing according to standard. Over the long run, performance standards eventually decline as workers observe that poor performance is not only acceptable, but also rewarded with a paycheck. Additionally, coworkers frequently need to perform extra work to compensate for the poor performers. Resentment mounts toward these poorly functioning employees as pride in the work diminishes. Anger and frustration increase towards management for failure to address the issue. Pride in performance, productivity, and quality all decline as a result of not holding people accountable. Does this sound familiar?

A new chief executive officer of a governmental organization sought my consulting services regarding a number of tough issues. This career change placed him in charge of an organization that, for many years, had tolerated poor performance. He quickly determined that a number of people were card-carrying members of the "walking dead" and had been permitted to perform poorly without being held accountable.

In deciding to deal with these non-performers, he met immediate resistance, even from some of his top management team: "You cannot do anything about these people. They are protected by Civil Service, their unions will resist your actions, they will file grievances, they...." The reasons for inaction accumulated.

The new chief executive listened to their excuses and decided to act in spite of the obstacles. "But," they protested, "it will take a year to deal with these people." "Where will we be in a year," he questioned, "if we do not do anything about these performance issues?"

Within one year, each one of these poor performers was either out of the organization or reassigned to a position that more appropriately matched his or her talents. No grievances resulted. No lawsuits. The tough-on-issues-and-tender-on-people manner in which he addressed the issues got the organization back on track. Productivity soared and pride returned. This executive demonstrated a courageous commitment to "Deliberate Success."

I continue to be amazed about how well it works when leaders are tough on issues and tender on people. Performed in the spirit of being authentic and "in service," coaching can facilitate employees to transform their performance from mediocre to masterful. The courage to address issues, coupled with coaching skills, can make a significant difference in enhancing both individual and team performance.

The coaching process, however, requires that the individual has the fundamental aptitude or talent to perform effectively in a given assignment. If the job requires the ability to "swim and fly," a duck fits the innate talent requirement. If the job requires "climbing trees," a squirrel fits the job well. Coaching a duck to climb trees or coaching a squirrel to swim and fly, however, results in a costly, unproductive experience. Managers in many organizations spend a disproportionate amount of time and resources "coaching" people who do not have the basic talent to do the job. Far greater productivity and fulfillment results from directing coaching efforts to your most talented people. Interestingly enough, talented people have far greater potential to perform at an even higher level than those who have a wide gap between where they are and where they need to be.[24]

The "best practice" principles, results-oriented strategies, and tangible coaching tools described here will support your efforts to enhance individual, team, and organizational effectiveness. By applying these tools, you will experience the benefit of building great teams that deliver impressive results.

"Stop trying to change people.
Start trying to help them
become more of who they already are."

—Marcus Buckingham

---

performance appraisal limitations

Most organizations require written performance appraisals at least once a year. Yet, I find that upper managers infrequently participate in the very performance evaluation process they require of others. Performance evaluations, as typically implemented, experience several major flaws:

- Performance evaluations often tend to focus on past weaknesses and shortcomings, making the review session itself a difficult experience for both the manager and associate.
- When linked to merit increases, an inherent conflict arises between determining the rewards an individual will receive and providing feedback for improved performance. Under these circumstances, associates often have reason to justify their past performance and present themselves in the best possible light to achieve favorable salary consideration.
- Managers tend to provide one-way, top-down feedback. Typically, the manager has 100 percent of the responsibility for the performance review, and the associate has no responsibility. This process fails to effectively engage the associate in looking at his own performance and in building internally driven accountability for enhancing his effectiveness.

Because of the stress and discomfort associated with the annual appraisal process, inherent conflict of interests, and focus on negatives, neither the manager nor the associate has an incentive to participate. With so few positive outcomes, it's no wonder people often ignore annual performance reviews. Coaching, on the other hand, provides an empowering, accountable alternative that actively engages associates in charting their future.

coaching: an empowering alternative

Coaching differs significantly from performance evaluation by focusing on the present and future rather than on the past. It is also a collaborative exchange rather than a top-down directive. Coaching clarifies direction, provides caring feedback, and encourages people to use their talents in service to the organization. Far broader in concept and application than traditional performance evaluations, coaching includes periodic performance appraisals as part of the overall process. It differs by actively engaging the associates in reinforcing strengths, clarifying targets, and encouraging stretches.

Effective coaching aligns individual and organizational vision and values while bringing out the best of each member of the team. Because coaching is *not* directly linked to compensation, associates tend to be more open and honest in assessing where they are now and where they need to be and in developing appropriate action plans to close the performance gap. In coaching, employees take greater accountability to enhance their own performance while managers add insight, guidance, and encouragement to the process.

Coaching has five primary applications, the first three of which are the most important and require your greatest efforts as you concentrate on your talented associates:

Primary focus of coaching (developing talent):
1. Teaching new skills.
2. Enhancing seasoned performance.
3. Grooming for new responsibilities.

Secondary focus of coaching (damage control):
4. Correcting poor performance.
5. Assisting others in finding a "career opportunity elsewhere."

In most organizations, managers spend 80 percent of their coaching efforts on damage control with a small number of marginal employees. This leaves only 20 percent of coaching time for developing talent for the majority of good workers. The best performers, on the other hand, have far greater potential and are far more responsive to effective coaching than are the marginal performers.[25] Which end of the continuum do you spend most of your time with: your best or your poorest employees? It seems that most organizations have this backward. Peak-performing organizations, however, place their resources where it counts: on the winners.

To achieve the best long-term results, consider the value of the following **10 Criteria for Successful Coaching**:

1. Actively engages the associate in self appraisal, emphasizing:
    *   Situation: Where am I now?
    *   Target: Where do I want to be?
    *   Proposal: How do I get there?
    *   Action Plan: What am I going to deliver by when?

2. Focuses on reinforcing or changing behaviors, not on changing the associate's personality.

3. Encourages a collaborative, two-way exchange in which both the manager and associate learn from each other about enhancing performance while building productive relationships.

4. Fosters mutual respect, open communication, and a spirit of partnership.

5. Emphasizes present and future performance. By putting the past aside, no need exists to siphon off creativity to defend former actions.

6. Aligns organizational with individual vision and values to enhance performance results.

7. Fosters personal accountability and self-management while reinforcing strengths and encouraging

performance stretches in serving organizational interests.

8. Provides ongoing exchanges to clarify expectations between the manager and associate regarding performance goals and measurable outcomes (the "deliverables").

9. Clarifies the job FAREs: Functions, Authority, Responsibilities, and Expectations to assure that talent is directed in service to the organization.

10. Provides ongoing feedback for both celebrating successes and taking corrective action to achieve the results you seek.

Effective coaching requires a safe, open environment for candid straight talk in addressing issues and in encouraging people to use their talents at the highest level. Caring straight talk and effective feedback provide the coaching vehicles for developing others. Amazing things can happen when people are on "speaking terms" with one another, and when you share your truth.

"I don't have a lot of respect for talent.
Talent is genetic.
It's what you do with it that counts."

—Martin Ritt

chapter 11

coaching straight talk:

the courage to speak
and the safety to listen

"There are two causes for all misunderstandings:
1. not saying what you mean,
and 2. not doing what you say."

—Angeles Arrien

COACHING—BRINGING OUT the best of others—requires that you talk straight with your associates. Improving performance depends on clear, timely, caring feedback that is tough on issues and tender on people. As an effective coach, you need to have the courage to speak "your truth" and to provide a safe environment to receive "their truth."

Many managers, however, find it hard to speak their truth—even though they know that people cannot improve their performance without effective feedback. So why do we sometimes avoid telling our truth? It might hurt the feelings of others. It's uncomfortable. It's stressful. And we might even get the truth back!

For whatever excuses, avoiding dealing with sensitive issues often results in those same issues becoming the proverbial 800-pound gorilla. Rather than dealing directly with sensitive issues, we dance around the point, drop indirect hints, avoid the issues, or become so diplomatic that no one has the slightest idea what we are talking about!

Frustrated and angry, a department head came into my office wanting my approval for him to immediately fire one of his poorly performing employees. The employee worked in the hospital for more than five years and had never been particularly effective. In fact, according to the department head, he periodically interrupted his mediocre performance with some rather serious mistakes. Two such blunders in the last week jeopardized patient safety and prompted the department head to finally take action.

When I asked what the employee knew about his chronic poor performance, the manager responded, "He has to know! He's been here for five years." Not finding that to be a satisfactory answer, I asked to see the employee's performance evaluations for the last five years. From the employee's personnel file, we pulled the five performance evaluations and placed them in chronological order in front of us on a conference table.

What do suppose they said about his performance for the past five years? You guessed it: Each annual performance appraisal reported overall ratings ranging from "satisfactory" to even as high as "outstanding." I said to the manager, "I don't understand how these evaluations can be as good as they are when you said his performance has been so poor all these years." After a long pause, the department head said quietly, "Well, I didn't want to hurt his feelings." I asked, "What do you suppose firing him will do to his feelings?"

We both learned from this experience. It became apparent to me that I needed to be clearer about my expectations of department directors to hold themselves and others accountable through clear, straight talk. He learned that avoiding issues and not shooting straight generally worsens the situation. How about you? What courageous conversations might you be avoiding—at work and at home? What consequences might you experience from not dealing directly with issues calling for attention? (By the way, in the interest of patient safety, we did terminate the employee.)

communication success criteria: courage and safety

Effective coaching requires an open communication exchange between the coach and the associate. Both safety in seeking the truth from others and courage in speaking your truth are essential in dealing with performance issues and in supporting personal and professional growth.

I feel "safe," for example, when I can candidly "be me" when I am with you. And for me to "be me" means that I can safely share what I am thinking, feeling, and wanting in a way that also honors the other person. Likewise, effective communication exchanges require the courage to both self-disclose and give honest feedback to others. Combining safety and courage in this context enables people to connect with far greater clarity and mutual understanding.

Unfortunately, many managers have difficulty in telling their truth about performance issues to employees in a timely, direct, and caring way. Performance issues are often ignored (tender on issues) or dealt with harshly (tough on people). Another common problem occurs when managers accumulate performance information on employees and then do a "data dump" during their annual appraisal.

Can you imagine a football coach observing his players in action throughout the season, keeping track of what they did well and what they did poorly, and then calling each player in at the end of the season to give them feedback about their annual performance? The "coach" would soon find himself looking for a new job. Whether in the corporate environment or on the playing field, quality, timely, constructive coaching provides the foundation for Deliberate Success. As Ken Blanchard frequently says, "Feedback is the breakfast of champions."

the 4 "truth tests"

For fear of telling "the truth," two kinds of lies are often shared during performance evaluations: distorting the truth and withholding the truth. The moment one distorts or withholds his or her truth, relationship separation begins, mutual understanding declines, and unproductive behaviors increase. The quality of an effective working relationship, therefore, is a function of how much truth is exchanged. Telling your truth, as you know it, greatly simplifies the communication process and takes the guesswork and game-playing out of relationships. Although I am not advocating "compulsive truth-telling," I am encouraging you to be both *authentic* (speaking your truth) and *in service* (meeting your interests and theirs) as a foundation for effective coaching.

Rather than have others guess how you evaluate their performance, you can assist their growth and development by reinforcing that which is going well and by dealing directly with the issues. If you are wondering whether it is advisable to deal with an issue, consider the following "truth tests," based largely on an ancient Asian philosophy:

1. **Is it true?** Be careful with this, for there are three "truths": "my truth," "their truth," and "The Truth."

What you believe to be "The Truth" may merely be your perception of The Truth.

2. **Is it kind and respectful to deal with the issue?** Consider not only the involved individual, but also others who may be affected by the situation. Sometimes *not* dealing with a situation is disrespectful to both the individual and to those indirectly involved.

3. **Is it necessary to confront the situation?** Consider the short- and long-term consequences of confronting—and of not confronting—issues requiring attention.

4. **Is it timely?** Being sensitive to timing in dealing with a situation can have a significant impact on the results achieved. In most cases, dealing with the situation close to the triggering event will more likely produce a positive outcome than will procrastinating.

"Be willing to tell your truth—sooner!"

—Alan Cohen

---

the 3 communication styles

People typically practice three communication styles: passive, aggressive, and assertive. You will likely be familiar with these in both your personal and professional experiences.

Passive or indirect communication forces the other person to guess about what you are really thinking, feeling, and wanting. Both tender on people and tender on issues, this indirect style avoids resolution and ultimately increases interpersonal tension and frustration.

The previously described story about the department director who wanted to fire the five-year hospital employee demonstrates passive communication. The employee had every right to assume that his performance was in fact satisfactory given his manager's inaccurate feedback. Because passive communication tends to both withhold and distort feedback, others find it hard to know for sure when someone is really telling the truth or merely walking through another communication facade. As a result, performance issues tend to worsen as employees become increasingly unaware of their unawareness! How can one be expected to improve performance if he does not receive honest feedback?

"Shovel while the piles are small!"

—Author unknown

Aggressive communication reflects the "I just tell it like it is—if they can't handle it, that's their problem" kind of attitude. This communication style damages relationships and even encourages recipients to shift their focus from their own performance issues to the unfair, insensitive manner in which they were addressed. The message gets lost because of the way in which the messenger delivered the feedback. The aggressive communicator will soon find himself alone.

Dealing with difficult performance matters requires sensitivity to The Human Element while dealing directly with the issues. Straight talk, or *assertive* communication, matches your outer expression (what you say) with your inner experience (what you are thinking, feeling, and wanting) while simultaneously treating others with respect. By talking straight in a caring way, you can separate the person from the issue or behavior. Caring straight talk and effective feedback provide the coaching vehicles for developing others. As you have already concluded, assertive communications combines the magic ingredients of simultaneously being tough on issues and tender on people.

Imagine I am your manager and we are meeting to discuss your performance. Having just talked about your strengths, I say to you, "Let's talk about your *weaknesses.*" What happens inside? Chances are, you become tense, your stomach tightens up, and you feel the need to withdraw. Or instead, you might want to thoroughly explore *my* weaknesses! This is not the best time to have a quality, open discussion about performance issues.

Now, imagine that once again I am your manager, and we are in a performance evaluation. We have just talked about your strengths, and I say to you, "Let's explore ways in which you can be *even more* effective, things that you can do *more of* and *less of* that will enhance your long-term effectiveness." Notice the difference in your internal response when we address these issues as "stretches" rather than weaknesses. If you are like most people, you feel more open, more receptive, and more willing to actively participate in generating ideas to enhance performance.

Not "sugarcoating" in any way, this approach deals directly, yet sensitively, with the issues while actively engaging the associate in the process of self-examination. People are much more likely to feel respected and to have ownership of the ideas emerging from this coaching strategy. This path directs creative energy to problem-solving and attaining performance results.

Negative issues are not ignored; instead, they are dealt with openly and in a caring way. Such respectful straight talk encourages the associate to join rather than resist you in the problem-solving process. People tend to support that which they assist to create. And you are more likely to achieve lasting, positive results when reinforcing strengths and addressing stretches with your associate.

When given in the spirit of being both authentic and in service, feedback is a gift. Coaching positions the team leader and the associate to give and receive valuable performance feedback intended to create even more effective organizational results while building career fulfillment.

Some less-than-secure managers, however, may be threatened by the thought of exposing themselves to such honest two-way communications. Some people insulate themselves from feedback, thus creating a closed, low-trust environment. Under these circumstances, "parking lot" meetings occur as communication channels erode and people look for other outlets to share what they are thinking, feeling, and wanting. People need to have the confidence that giving feedback to another person is safe and not subject to future reprisals—in any form.

"Seek first to understand, then to be understood."

—**St. Francis of Assisi**

---

breaking through the communication barrier: tools to apply safety and courage

Effective communication can occur only when people have the courage to speak their truth while simultaneously providing safety to others in sharing their truth. If the communication environment lacks either courage or safety, immediate blocks occur. So, how do you create more safety in the communication process? The following five steps facilitate connection and understanding in even the most difficult of interpersonal circumstances: [26]

1. **Pause.** When receiving difficult feedback, people often engage in their own self-talk or interrupt the

communication process. Instead, pause and prepare yourself for active listening. Not just a brief "time-out," pausing enables you to get quiet and centered rather than to react. Pausing deliberately engages your internal resources by tapping into what you intuitively know and using that at a higher level. Pausing intentionally brings out your best, rather than your baggage!

2. **Say, "Tell me more."** Asking for more feedback—even when you don't even like what you are hearing—appears counterintuitive and possibly even self-deprecating. Encouraging people to talk *with* you rather than *about* you, however, creates a safe climate for exploring even the most sensitive of issues. Providing this degree of open communication discourages "parking lot" meetings and encourages straight talk.

3. **Listen with every bone in your body.** Rather than listening, many of us are just waiting to talk, preparing our rebuttal, or rearranging our prejudices. None of these are listening. And remember: Active listening is one of the highest forms of respecting others.

4. **Find a way to understand their facts, their feelings, and their perceptions.** Even though you might not agree with the speaker, your present-moment mission is to seek understanding. Understanding builds respect, facilitates problem-solving, enables you to connect, and also positions you to later be understood.

5. **Reward the feedback.** Although you may not like or agree with the feedback, encourage your associate to continue open dialogue about even the most sensitive

of issues. Say something such as, "Thank you. That helps me to better understand your concerns and interests." A simple "thank you" promotes positive and timely exchanges.

In a session that Stephen Covey and I facilitated with a client of mine, he introduced yet another effective tool designed to promote and encourage positive exchanges. When in conflict, Dr. Covey proposed asking the following question: "Are you willing to engage in dialogue until we come up with a win-win solution?" What a powerful question! This strategy fosters a spirit of partnership to cocreate options for mutual gain. Whether problem-solving, conflict resolution, or working through performance issues, this key question, coupled with the five-step method of providing communication safety, positions people to understand one another and to cocreate mutually beneficial outcomes.

In contrast, note how the following true story created a condition of fear in the work environment:

A city government client of mine experienced considerable problems within the fire department. Low trust levels, guarded communications, and fragmented teamwork characterized the organizational culture.

The fire chief said to me, "I used to get a lot of negative feedback about how things are going around here. I don't get that feedback anymore. Things must be going better." His conclusion ignored reality!

After interviewing each of his battalion chiefs and station captains, I learned that things were not going well at all. In fact, a near-mutiny was in progress.

How could he have been so out of touch? Feedback from his leadership team provided a sobering reality check. At a meeting he called with his team, he reportedly said, "I want to get to the bottom of this once and for all. What's going on in the department?" After some hesitation, a courageous captain raised his hand and proceeded to give the chief feedback—feedback he did not like to hear. The chief interrupted him, pointed his finger at the captain, and said, "You! Out in the hall!" He ordered the captain out in the hall as the other members of the leadership team watched in disbelief!

For some reason, people stopped talking directly to the chief. But they didn't stop talking about him. Instead of "parking lot" meetings, the firefighters had "kitchen table" meetings about the chief—and the chief was the main course for breakfast, lunch, and dinner.

Some managers just don't get how important it is to create a safe environment for constructive feedback. The chief's single action of ordering a captain out in the hall solidified how unsafe it is to communicate with him. Anyone with an IQ of two or less would know how inappropriate his actions were. Yet, many of us have done things to cut off open communications at work and at home—equivalent to saying, "You! Out in the hall." Managers who don't provide safety for open communications shoot themselves in the foot and admire their aim!

In addition to providing safety, effective coaching requires the courage to speak your truth, especially as it relates to the following:

1. **Be willing to self-disclose** about what you are thinking, wanting, and feeling—especially regarding matters that count. Don't expect people to read your mind. Demonstrate the courage to state your needs and interests clearly, respectfully, and on a timely basis.

2. **Be willing to give performance feedback** to others about your observations and expectations. In particular, your

coaching effectiveness can be enhanced by reinforcing strengths, encouraging "stretches," and clarifying the performance targets and goals of your associates.

"Successful people make progress while unsuccessful people make excuses."

—Brian Tracy

---

v-a-k feedback: communicating with clarity and precision

Have you ever had the experience of giving what you thought was crystal-clear feedback to someone only to later discover he or she didn't have a clue what you meant? Perhaps you have had this happen both at work and at home. I certainly have.

When giving feedback regarding The Human Element, avoid such ambiguities as "you need to improve your attitude" or "you need to be more respectful of others." These vague terms are subject to a broad range of interpretations. Behavior-Specific Feedback, instead, will more likely be understood when put into actionable terms. This kind of feedback, coming from the study of neurolinguistic programming (NLP), converts a somewhat intangible concept (such as "respect") into actionable behaviors (how do I *do* respect?).

By effectively describing behavioral expectations in terms of what do those behaviors look like (visual), sound like (auditory), and feel like (kinesthetic), people can more readily convert the intangible concepts into tangible results. If you are coaching a manager to be more "respectful," for example, apply the following V-A-K (Visual-Auditory-Kinesthetic) communication tools to assure understanding of your expectations:

VISUAL: What does "respect" *look* like? I *see* you:
- Showing up to meetings on time.
- Periodically having lunch with staff members.
- Making rounds and connecting more often.
- Acknowledging others through tangible memos and cards.

AUDITORY: What does "respect" *sound* like? I *hear* you:
- Publicly acknowledging successes of others.
- Asking for others' ideas and advice.
- Thanking people for their contributions.
- Listening more than talking.
- Encouraging others to take risks.
- Asking for what people learned when making a mistake.
- Providing coaching feedback.
- Seeking to draw the answers out of others.

KINISTHETIC: What does "respect" *feel* like? Around you, people *feel*:
- Safe and self-assured.
- A willingness to share even sensitive feedback, knowing that it will not come back to haunt them.
- A sense of partnership and connection, both when you are around and absent.

I have found that direct V-A-K feedback, given in the spirit of being in service and being authentic, facilitates a meaningful dialogue in even the most sensitive of situations. People stay with you, understand the message, and are more likely to join you in cocreating a behavioral action plan for improving their performance. Clarifying behavioral expectations in terms of what you would like to see, hear, and feel facilitates understanding and positions the associate to act with greater certainty. Through awareness, more effective choices can be made to enhance results.

---

communicating for understanding:
converting intangible concepts into actionable behaviors

visual:
what do the desired behaivors *look* like?

v-a-k
behavior-specific
feedback

auditory:
what do the desired behaviors *sound* like?

kinesthetic:
what do the desired behaviors *feel* like?

Effective coaching requires that you be tough on issues and tender on people. Having the courage to share your truth while providing safety to others to speak their truth positions both of you to better understand one another, clarify expectations, and work together toward mutual solutions.

If you were to ask your associates to describe your communication effectiveness, how would they respond? What can you do differently to achieve even better performance results? Rather than giving an example, be the example you seek from others. As you coach others, demonstrate the courage to speak your truth with care and the safety to encourage others to speak their truth.

"Communicating clearly is like using a phone number—you need all the digits to get through. If you leave a number out or put the area code at the end, see what happens. If communications is a phone number, intent is the area code."

—Rick Brinkman

chapter 12

coaching strategies and tools:

achieving performance results

*"To achieve things that you have never achieved before,
you must be willing to do things that you have never done before."*

—Author unknown

COACHING PROVIDES TANGIBLE tools to get from where you are to where you want to be. When integrated into the culture of an organization, ongoing coaching brings out the passion of people, empowers them to use their talents in service to converting your vision into reality, and engages their spirit to perform at their best. Your ongoing investment in coaching delivers a high rate of return.

Virtually every contact with employees provides an opportunity for coaching in the context of open, honest, caring communications. In bringing out the best of your associates, look for and create opportunities to reinforce their strengths, encourage their "stretches," and clarify their performance targets.

This chapter will provide you with numerous, user-friendly tools to both bring out the best of your associates and to deal with the difficult stuff. Each of the following coaching tools explored here can be immediately applied in achieving the results you are seeking. Here are the coaching tools you will be addressing:

1. S-S-T (Strength-Stretch-Target) Performance Coaching.
2. Partnership Coaching.
3. Peer Coaching.
4. Process-Improvement Coaching.
5. Coaching When Things "Hit the Fan."
6. Career Coaching.
7. Termination Coaching.

s-s-t (strength-stretch-target) performance coaching

Periodic formal coaching sessions have similarities with, yet significant differences from, performance evaluations. Performance evaluations utilize mostly top-down communications, focus on the past, and rarely engage the associate in meaningful dialogue. In typical performance evaluations, managers itemize associates' past "rights and wrongs." The S-S-T coaching process, on the other hand, safely engages associates in the self-exploration process of *drawing* out their:

Strengths: Where am I now?
Stretches: How do I get to where I need to be?
Targets: What performance goals am I seeking?

This S-S-T coaching process, unlike performance evaluations, places *80 percent* of the responsibility on the associate and only *20 percent* on the manager. This shift of accountability enhances self-awareness and facilitates addressing sensitive issues. In this S-S-T Performance Coaching process, both manager and associate focus on Strengths, Stretches, and Targets related to honoring that which is going well, identifying opportunities for enhancement, and clarifying expectations. Associates develop their own S-S-Ts and prepare performance action plans for discussion with their manager, including:

Strengths: What am I doing particularly well?
- The Bottom-Line Factors: productivity, knowledge, skills, and quality.
- The Human-Element Factors: relationships, attitude, and team strengths.

Stretches: To enhance my effectiveness, what can I do: (on The Bottom Line and The Human Element)
- More of or start doing?
- Less of or stop doing?

Targets: What outcomes and performance goals am I seeking to achieve on both The Bottom Line and The Human Element to enhance individual and organizational excellence?

Prior to conducting a formal coaching session, both the manager and the associate prepare to ensure an optimum outcome. The associate might benefit by taking several days to reflect on and complete her own S-S-T plan, after which she schedules a one-hour appointment with the manager to work through her S-S-Ts in a coaching session. Both the manager and the associate benefit by preparing for the following:

1. What do I want to accomplish?
   A. Strengths to reinforce?
   B. Stretches to encourage?
   C. Targets to clarify?
2. What high-priority stretches do I need to address and what measurable outcomes do I need to include in my performance enhancement plan?
3. What follow-up steps will assure positive outcomes?

4. What can my manager and I do more of and less
    of to enhance our working relationship?

Will associates be honest in their S-S-T performance plan? I
have found that a significant majority of employees are even
tougher on themselves than would be their managers. Sometimes,
however, people are either unaware of some their own issues or
deliberately attempt to distort their strengths and stretches. At
this "teachable moment," application of caring, straight-talk principles by the manager assists in delivering an appropriate "wake-
up call" to the associate.

If an associate misses something significant about his or her
performance, an opportunity presents itself to ask: "May I share
an observation that may be outside of your awareness?" Two
benefits result from this approach. First, by asking "permission"
to make a sensitive observation, the associate feels respected
and even empowered to exercise more control over their personal environment. (I have never had someone refuse this re-
quest.) Second, this approach presents a "face-saving" method
of dealing with an important issue requiring attention.

Growth requires quality feedback—both for you and your
associate. Behavioral changes are more likely to occur by positively presenting coaching feedback close to the triggering event
and then following up. When coaching individuals through significant stretches, set up at least two specific follow-up dates for
the purposes of celebrating successes and identifying next steps
for personal and professional development. Setting up these
meetings in advance provides subtle stress to perform and demonstrates your commitment to achieving results.

The manager should also prepare to openly discuss observations of the associate's S-S-Ts to assure both agree on important
issues. A simple system of classifying priorities on a scale of zero
to 10 greatly enhances understanding while encouraging appropriate behavioral emphasis. Critically important stretches are

identified as a nine or 10; issues of lessor importance might call for a ranking of only two or three.

Finally, managers should be prepared to discuss their strengths and stretches related to working with the associate. This coaching session provides a great opportunity to explore:

- **Strengths:** As your manager, what am I doing that works particularly well in my relationship with you?
- **Stretches:** What can I do more of and less of that will enhance the effectiveness of our working relationship?
- **Targets:** What performance outcomes can we mutually agree to that will produce even better results?

Engaging in this discussion, as risky as it may sound, builds trust, clarifies expectations, and enhances working relationships. Leaders who participate in this process, over the long run, create giants of others while marshaling forces to produce even greater results for the organization.

Refer to the S-S-T Performance Coaching Profile illustration at the right. A performance graph assists both you and your associate to visualize performance on two

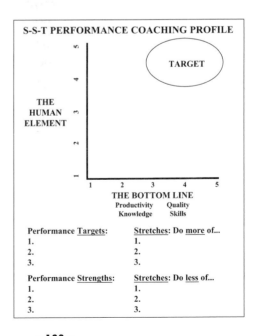

important elements: The Bottom Line and The Human Element. The Bottom Line (horizontal axis) focuses on several performance criteria: productivity, quality, knowledge, and skills.

Examining "The Bottom Line" performance factors first, identify where you see your associate's performance on these combined criteria, recognizing that actual performance may differ with each criterion. (Your associate will also be completing this coaching document. Advance preparation, however, will help position you for a successful outcome.) The combined or composite point total for The Bottom Line (on a scale of one to five) provides a clear starting point for discussion with your associate.

The Human Element reflects a more ambiguous, intangible dimension of performance descriptors than do The Bottom Line factors. Although undeniably important, The Human Element frequently presents a challenge to effectively describe. More often than not, terminations, transfers, and demotions occur because of interpersonal issues rather than bottom line skill factors. A 10-year study by the Carnegie Foundation concluded that approximately 90 percent of performance issues result from interpersonal incompetence, not technical incompetence.

On a scale of one to five, rank your associate on the vertical axis or The Human Element. At the *upper* end of the scale, you will likely experience such behaviors as: respectful of others; open, effective communicator; team player; builds positive relationships with others; aware; practices win-win conflict; trustworthy and trusting; empowers others; easy or safe to be with; flexible; creative; accountable; and empowering of others.

At the *lower* end of The Human Element scale, behaviors are more likely to be disrespectful, unaccountable, blaming, and "unsafe" for open communications. Additionally, guarded behaviors, hidden agendas, poor conflict-management skills, and poor teamwork typically emerge at the lower level of The Human Element scale.

Identifying a coordinate point that connects The Bottom Line and The Human Element creates a visual display of current performance factors and facilitates open communications regarding the gap between where the individual is now and where he needs to be for even more effective performance. One can *see* his performance status on the graphic display, *hear* quality feedback coming from you, and *feel* the effects of his performance. (The previously described V-A-K sensory specific feedback will provide clarity and build understanding.)

As an alternative to identifying a particular performance coordinate on the S-S-T Coaching Profile, you might consider drawing a "performance zone." Because performance, even with the same individual, varies from day to day, a "performance zone" may more appropriately describe his

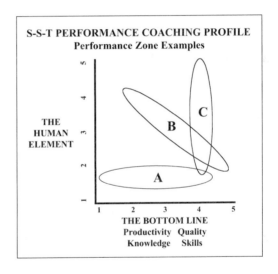

range of performance. Consider the following "performance zone" examples of several "behavioral challenges."

associate "a" performance zone observations

This performance zone suggests that the individual has significant productivity and quality variations. At times, he performs well in achieving tangible results. On other occasions, however, both quality and productivity suffer. He has consistently poor interpersonal relations and seems to attract conflict. When coaching him, focus on enhancing interpersonal relationships while developing performance and quality consistency on The Bottom Line.

This individual presents a particular challenge because he lacks interpersonal and team-development skills and simultaneously provides inconsistent productivity and quality. One needs to assess whether or not this person is an appropriate fit in this job. Unless significant miracles take place in the coaching process, this person is a strong candidate for "experiencing a career opportunity elsewhere."

associate "b" performance zone observations

This performance zone visually describes an unusual behavioral pattern that some would consider "crazy making!" When performing at the upper ranges on The Human Element, this manager has significant difficulty in achieving bottom-line results. She exhibits friendliness, connection with others, and concern for their welfare. At the same time, she holds neither herself nor others accountable for achieving and sustaining The Bottom Line results related to quality, performance, and profitability.

When pressure to perform on The Bottom Line occurs (usually from her boss), she will likely exhibit an abrupt personality change. She becomes demanding, insensitive, calculating, and highly results-oriented. Clearly, this person has not learned how to integrate The Human Element with The Bottom Line. She is an "either/or" practitioner; either she addresses The Bottom Line *or* The Human Element. When coaching this individual, consistently link The Human Element with The Bottom Line. This person needs to develop self-awareness, skills in bringing out the best of people, and achieving tangible results.

associate "c" performance zone observations

This associate performs exceptionally well on The Bottom Line, yet is subject to wide variations on The Human Element. He works hard, achieves high productivity results, and demonstrates task competence.

Although technically competent, this individual has significant mood swings that impact the productivity of others. When he's hot, he's hot. When he's not, he's not! People often have to "walk on eggshells" when around him. If others need to interact with him on a particular day, they will benefit by checking his "mood barometer" with other associates to determine how safe it is to either be around him or to make a proposal for his consideration. On a bad-mood day, people learn to stay clear or suffer the consequences.

When coaching this individual, reinforce his ability to achieve results. Yet, at the same time, clarify expectations related to his ability to create a safe environment, build a spirit of partnership, and foster open communications. His mood swings create hidden organizational costs that are likely outside of his awareness. He will likely be defensive about his own productivity and miss how his behavior diminishes teamwork and synergy.

linking s-s-t performance zones with v-a-k feedback

The following case study, involving a chief operating officer of a high-tech firm, provides a clear understanding of how a performance zone can be useful in addressing strengths, stretches, and targets.

A chief operating officer (COO) performed moderately well on The Bottom Line, yet poorly on The Human Element. Morale hit rock bottom as productivity continued to decline. His task orientation and inattention to people gradually alienated the staff. Employee relations continued to deteriorate as his style demonstrated a distinct lack of respect for the employees.

The COO, in the eyes of his employees, demonstrated a lack of respect by such behaviors as consistently showing up late to meetings, not listening, and berating employees in front of others when they made mistakes. Additionally, he typically failed to acknowledge successes of others while isolating himself in his office. Finally, he excelled in his ability to criticize others.

His boss, the company president, attempted to deal with the COO's situation through annual performance evaluations. For eight consecutive years, the president communicated the message "I want you to respect people more." A large bonus check also accompanied each of the performance evaluations. For some reason, the COO did not change his behaviors!

Out of desperation, the president asked for my assistance in dealing with this issue. In meeting privately with the president, I asked him utilize the S-S-T Performance Coaching Profile in evaluating the COO's performance. Not surprisingly, he identified the COO as "3.5" on The Bottom Line and "2" on The Human Element. The COO's performance contradicted rather than supported the organization's stated values.

I then met with the COO and requested that he identify how he saw himself on the S-S-T Performance Coaching Profile. Given the bonuses he had received over the past eight years, I understood when he saw himself as "4" on The Bottom Line and "4" on The Human Element. The gap between how he saw himself and how the

*president saw him resulted in significant tension for years
between the two top leaders.*

*My next step included getting the president and the
COO together to share their results. When comparing
the two S-S-T Performance Coaching Profiles, the COO
responded with shock and anger. Although he was clearly
surprised, this "wake-up call" created the foundation
for a higher level of understanding and clarification of
performance expectations.*

How could the two of them have been so different in their
performance assessments? First, the president historically did
not have the courage to address the issues directly. Second, the
COO did not make it safe for others to give him honest feedback. Third, the general charge of "I want you to respect people
more" lacked clarity of direction and did not provide a high
level of understanding between the two.

At that point, I introduced the V-A-K Behaviorally Specific
Feedback to the COO as a means to clarify what the desired
behaviors look like, sound like, and feel like. Only when he understood how to translate the concept of respect into specific
behaviors did significant progress occur. We identified a number of tangible, action-oriented behaviors that demonstrate "doing" respect.

The following performance "stretch" commitments emerged
from the COO once he understood how to convert the concept
of respect into action through V-A-K Behaviorally Specific Feedback:

To respect others, I will do *more of* or start doing the following:

- Show up to meetings on time.
- Listen 75 percent; talk 25 percent.
- Provide positive feedback regularly.

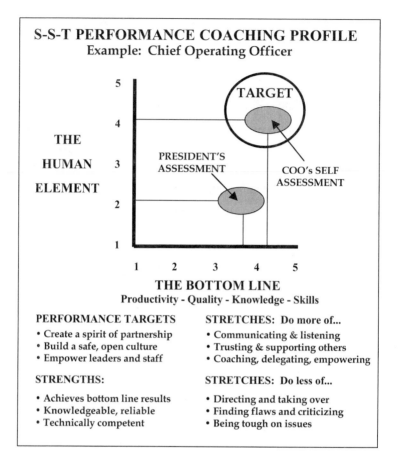

S-S-T PERFORMANCE COACHING PROFILE
Example: Chief Operating Officer

THE

HUMAN

ELEMENT

TARGET

PRESIDENT'S
ASSESSMENT

COO's SELF
ASSESSMENT

THE BOTTOM LINE
Productivity - Quality - Knowledge - Skills

PERFORMANCE TARGETS

• Create a spirit of partnership
• Build a safe, open culture
• Empower leaders and staff

STRENGTHS:

• Achieves bottom line results
• Knowledgeable, reliable
• Technically competent

STRETCHES: Do more of...

• Communicating & listening
• Trusting & supporting others
• Coaching, delegating, empowering

STRETCHES: Do less of...

• Directing and taking over
• Finding flaws and criticizing
• Being tough on issues

- Commit to coaching others periodically.
- Celebrate successes publicly.
- Criticize privately.
- Support creative ideas.
- Look for the learning when mistakes are made.
- Build rapport and support.
- Balance my task orientation with greater sensitivity to The Human Element.

To respect others, I will do *less of* or stop doing the following:

- Find the flaws in the ideas of others.
- Criticize individuals publicly.
- Abandon people when they make a mistake.

For the first time, he began to understand how to convert the concept of respect into specific, tangible behaviors. Behaviorally Specific Feedback enables an intangible concept (such as respect) to be understood in concrete, behavioral actions. By clarifying expectations, the probability of achieving desired results significantly increases.

self-directed s-s-t coaching process

Shifting coaching responsibility from the manager to the associate, as previously addressed, positions associates to assume higher levels of accountability in addressing their career development. Extensive experience in many organizations demonstrates the value of this self-directed coaching process. In the long run, associates play a far more active role in charting their future, experience a higher degree of ownership, and tend to sustain higher levels of performance. Because people tend to support that which they help to create, both the associates and the organization benefit from this self-directed coaching tool.

Let's examine another tangible S-S-T Performance Coaching application. The following example involves a director of public relations whose "performance zone" shines on The Human Element, yet suffers on The Bottom Line. Like before, charge him with preparing his own S-S-Ts for a coaching session with you. Through the process of self-examination, tough issues tend to be desensitized while encouraging personal accountability and self-management.

In this self-directed coaching process, he assumes 80 percent of the responsibility for self-assessment and development of a professional growth plan. Your 20 percent of the responsibility involves clarification expectations in behaviorally specific

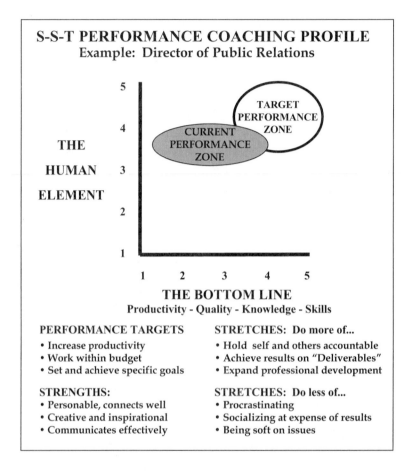

S-S-T PERFORMANCE COACHING PROFILE
Example: Director of Public Relations

THE HUMAN ELEMENT

TARGET PERFORMANCE ZONE

CURRENT PERFORMANCE ZONE

THE BOTTOM LINE
Productivity - Quality - Knowledge - Skills

PERFORMANCE TARGETS
• Increase productivity
• Work within budget
• Set and achieve specific goals

STRETCHES: Do more of...
• Hold self and others accountable
• Achieve results on "Deliverables"
• Expand professional development

STRENGTHS:
• Personable, connects well
• Creative and inspirational
• Communicates effectively

STRETCHES: Do less of...
• Procrastinating
• Socializing at expense of results
• Being soft on issues

terms to reinforce Strengths, encourage Stretches, and clarify Targets. Once achieving a high level of understanding, plan on at least two follow-up sessions to sustain positive performance results. Set the follow-up dates at the first coaching session.

S-S-T coaching positions individuals, teams, and ultimately organizations to prosper in a highly competitive environment. The commitment to ongoing renewal and reinvention taps into the best of each person and supports pride in performance.

partnership coaching:
building positive working relationships

Have you ever had "stuff" between you and another person that resulted in relationship tension? Of course you have. The costs of not dealing with issues include increased stress, impaired communications, and reduced productivity. Partnership Coaching provides a pragmatic tool for working through these issues with accountability and creating more favorable results.

Having taken thousands of executives and teams through Partnership Coaching over the years, I have found this to be one of the more effective means of enhancing communications and facilitating productive team behaviors. When integrated into the culture, Partnership Coaching provides an effective tool in elevating teams from good to great!

Identify an individual with whom you want to enhance working relationships with and invite him to participate with you in this five-step Partnership Coaching process. You and your "partner" then talk through each step before advancing to subsequent steps.[27]

1. strengths: the strengths i appreciate about you are....

This step provides an opportunity to express genuine appreciation to your associate for his strengths and contributions, even recognizing that relationship tension may exist between the two of you. Pausing to recognize his positive qualities assists in creating a more favorable atmosphere to address issues. After you share what you appreciate about him, he shares what he appreciates about you before both of you move on to the next step.

2. accountability: what I do that may get in the way of our working relationship is....

This conscious shift from blaming to personal accountability creates a new paradigm that facilitates self-reflection and encourages a more positive exchange. So what do you do that gets in the way? Perhaps withhold feedback, "parking lot" meetings, find the flaw in their ideas, or even premature closure? You honesty will encourage similar open disclosure and accountability.

3. strengths: to enhance the quality of our working relationship, i would like to see you:

A. Do *more of* or *start* doing the following....
B. Do *less of* or *stop* doing the following....

This step encourages clarification of expectations and focuses on present and future interests rather than recycling past transgressions.

4. commitments: to enhance our relationship, i intend to:

A. Do *more of* or *start* doing the following....
B. Do *less of* or *stop* doing the following....

After clarifying what each expects of the other, partners are now positioned to make a behavioral commitment. In addition to sharing verbally, each individual maintains a written record of the agreement to review in a follow-up session.

5. reinforcement: what else i appreciate about you is....

With rare exception, participants discover additional qualities they genuinely appreciate about the other when practicing this form of caring straight talk. Frequently, this process facilitates healing, encourages open communications, and enables people to get on with their work without the former relationship tension that detracted from quality performance.

The five-step Partnership Coaching tool provides just a bit of structure to facilitate two people talking through issues requiring attention. The process requires both a courageous and safe exchange that is tough as nails on issues, yet tender on people. If you find yourself straying off the subject during this exchange, pause and self-correct; you are likely avoiding the courageous conversation that needs to take place.

To achieve lasting results, I encourage participants to set at least two follow-up sessions, four and eight weeks after the first Partnership Coaching session. The follow-up provides an opportunity to both celebrate successes and seek additional ways to constructively enhance your working relationship. The built-in follow-up meetings apply "creative stress" to perform consistently with each partner's agreement.

The Partnership Coaching tool also facilitates relationship-building between individuals who already have a great kinship and want to make it even better. This same process can also be applied at home with your spouse and with your children. Having had direct, personal experience in applying Partnership Coaching in my own family, I can attest to the value of applying this tool to enhance already good relationships. Look for opportunities to use this important coaching tool at work and at home. (Note: I am *not* advocating conducting a performance evaluation on your spouse!)

peer coaching: enhancing individual and team effectiveness

Peer coaching and 360-degree feedback methods require high levels of trust and open communications to achieve productive outcomes. This Peer Coaching process provides yet another effective method of acquiring "growth feedback" to strengthen individual and team performance. Generally, a facilitator external to the team introduces this coaching process in an effort to build competence and confidence in giving and receiving feedback. An external facilitator initially creates a climate of safety while the team gains experience in this coaching process they will later manage on their own without external support.

Periodically, the team assembles to assess how they are functioning on both The Bottom Line and The Human Element. Team members both give and receive peer coaching feedback to one another about their perceived strengths and stretches. The simple, yet effective process includes the following steps in small groups of five or six coworkers:

step 1: self-assessment.

Associates describe how they contribute to team performance:

A. **Strengths**: "The major strengths that I bring to this team include...."
B. **Stretches**: "I could enhance my effectiveness on this team by doing *more of* and *less of* the following...."

step 2: listening to feedback from others.

The speaker then listens while the other team members provide the following coaching feedback:

A. **Strengths**: "What I appreciate about you is...."
B. **Stretches**: "To enhance your effectiveness on this team, I encourage you to do *more of* and *less of* the following...."

As a result of Peer Coaching, teams accelerate progress in enhancing interpersonal working relationships while achieving higher performance results. They learn how to keep things current between one another rather than accumulate additional baggage. They learn how to encourage one another while being tough and tender. And they learn how to work together far more effectively in accomplishing team goals while building job fulfillment—not bad outcomes!

"Never let your good get in the way of your better."

—Jack Bolen

---

process-improvement coaching: moving from good to great!

Moving from good to great requires a relentless pursuit of self-examination, process examination, and product examination. "Good enough" becomes the enemy of what could be even better. In this global economy, acceptance of "good enough" allows your competitors to gain the upper hand.

A still popular battle cry among second-string companies is "if it ain't broke, don't fix it!" (Is there any question why they are "second-string?") This "leave well enough alone" philosophy discourages entrepreneurial thinking and assumes that products, services, quality, and performance cannot be improved.

"If it ain't broke, *break* it" wrote Robert Kriegel in his book having the same title.[28] In my experience in working with peak-performance organizations, they assemble their team to critique a well-executed project (something that "ain't broke") and tear it apart in an effort to make it even better. This process involves two team-coaching questions:

1. **Strengths**: How did we achieve such great results?
2. **Stretches**: What could we have done differently to produce even better results?

When exploring **strengths**, I encourage team members to name names regarding who did what in achieving such outstanding results. Acknowledging results-oriented behaviors rewards people while encouraging others to strive for similar achievements the next time around. When addressing "**stretches**," I have found it helpful to identify behaviors, methods, and actions (not people) that could have produced even better results.

This Process-Improvement Coaching raises the performance bar and creates an environment that empowers others to be their best. People look forward to this Process-Improvement Coaching process while benefiting from the learning. Leading your team from good to great sometimes requires "breaking" something that "ain't broke."

coaching when things "hit the fan"

"The key to the ninety-nine is the one—
how you treat the one
reveals how you regard the 99
because everyone is ultimately one."

—Stephen Covey

Some things do break, however, and require repairs or replacement. When the situation involves people, your skill level in handling difficult situations will be tested. Evaluating a poorly executed project, assessing a product failure, or debriefing serious mistakes can be an important mechanism for learning, self-correcting, and reinforcing achievement of Deliberate Success. An IBM experience clearly demonstrates this point:

> *It seems that a young executive made an error that cost IBM 10 million dollars. Mr. Thomas Watson, then-president of IBM, invited the executive into his office to discuss the mistake. The vice president quietly said, "I*

suppose you want my resignation." Mr. Watson replied, "You must be kidding. We have ten million dollars invested in your education!"

Imagine the commitment of that young man to IBM at that point. It probably took him all of four days to come up with ideas to earn that money back! While interviewing a nine-year IBM veteran and discussing that story, he said to me, *"We don't punish people for making mistakes. If we did, all that we would teach them is to not take risks. We can't afford that."*

Another organization I am familiar with makes it particularly safe for individuals who make mistakes. The president has a bell in his office that associates ring when they make a mistake! In that culture, ringing the bell signals a time to pause to laugh and learn. They support the individual by laughing at the mistake, then seek the learning as a means of encouraging even higher levels of performance. On the other hand, failure to ring the bell will likely result in experiencing a career opportunity elsewhere! This culture supports growth and learning, not cover-up and non-accountability. How safe is it for people to "ring the bell" in your organization?

In contrast to creating a safe learning environment, some ineffective managers instead attempt to find culprits and nail them to the wall. When taken to an extreme, flaw-finding encourages employees to take lower risks and channels their creativity to focus on covering their tails rather than self-correcting. One client president of mine once said to his management team, *"I want you to take risks, and you better not make any mistakes!"* Needless to say, I had my challenges in coaching him.

The only true failure occurs when people do not learn from their mistakes. Edison would never have succeeded in creating the light bulb if he were sidetracked by the thousands of "failures" experienced in its development. Each "failure" provided important information that drew him closer to a successful result.

> "If you want to increase your success rate,
> double your failure rate."
>
> —Thomas Watson, Sr., Founder of IBM

When things do not go well, an incredible coaching opportunity arises to position your team for future success. When experiencing a temporary setback, assemble your team members to evaluate the situation and learn from the experience. In the spirit of being tough on issues and tender on people, explore the following key assessment elements:

1. **Strengths**: Even though we did not accomplish the intended outcomes, what did we do well? (Look closely, as strengths are usually present even in these circumstances.)
2. **Stretches**: To achieve great results in the future, what we can we do differently?
3. **Partnerships**: When experiencing temporary setbacks such as this, how can we support one another to encourage growth and creative thinking while fulfilling organizational needs?

In your organization, what specific actions are you taking to encourage positive self-evaluation when mistakes occur? How you deal with mistakes can provide magic coaching moments to build confidence, competence, and trust—while taking your team from good to great.

> "Success is going from failure to failure
> without loss of enthusiasm."
>
> —Winston Churchill

how to coach someone
who needs to leave the company

Can you think of an individual who is "retired on the job," a chronic poor performer, a poor fit, or one who simply does not have the innate talent to perform well in a given position? You have probably had the experience of interacting with such individuals at one point or another in your career. Whether a colleague, an employee responsible to you, or even your boss, the experience of working with a "wild goose" that will not or cannot fly in formation is universally frustrating.

If an individual flies in a different direction or functions outside the corporate values or performance standards, you have a distinct responsibility to deal with the situation. Discovering why someone performs outside the standards provides you with important information about what strategies to use in dealing effectively with the performance challenge. Some of the more common reasons for not "flying in formation" include:

- Not aligning with the corporate direction or values (assuming appropriate ethical standards).
- Not willing (attitude) or able (aptitude) to perform consistent with the standards.
- Not being a team player or not having a positive attitude.
- Not being sufficiently trained or oriented into the position.
- Not keeping up with professional or technological developments.
- Not having appropriate system, equipment, or support services.

- Not having sufficient direction and feedback for him to know he is flying in formation.
- Not having a strong sense of personal accountability and commitment to address his performance issues.

Talk with the individual to find out the reasons for his lack of performance. The intent is to inspire him, not fire him. Coach him to deal with the cause, not just the effects. If he cannot or will not consistently perform with the corporate vision, values, and standards, the job fit is not good, and he needs to move on.

When an individual performs poorly, you are responsible for working with him to assure that he meets company expectations. Empowerment does not include allowing individuals to operate outside the context of the organizational vision, values, and standards. When an individual exhibits poor performance, you have three options:

- **Option 1:** *Relax* your performance standards to make it officially acceptable for substandard performers to stay on board. (Be careful of using this strategy! Although it has obvious and significant drawbacks, you will be amazed how many managers lack the courage to deal directly with the non-performance issue.)
- **Option 2:** *Reaffirm* the corporate vision, values, and performance standards and coach the individual to rise to the appropriate performance expectations.
- **Option 3:** *Release* the poor performer by giving him a "career opportunity elsewhere."

A fourth option—the transfer of a poor performer to a position in which he or she will do the "least amount of harm"— sounds like an easy way out. This practice, however, systematically reduces company pride and conveys the message that I don't think you want to send. Never, never, never transfer problem performers! Have the courage to deal with the performance issue and, instead, use transfers to consciously broaden organizational skills and to develop the talents of qualified individuals.

Because most organizations are not driven by some social service philosophy designed to give jobs to incompetent people, allowing substandard performance discourages that person and others from functioning at their best. In the long run, not dealing with substandard performance actually disempowers a significant chunk of employees who conclude that poor performance is not only acceptable, but that it qualifies employees for full compensation!

The president of a service organization invited me to work with him regarding how to deal with his general manager. Although the general manager performed adequately on The Bottom Line, he disempowered and alienated people at all levels in the organization. Organizational performance started to decline as The Human Element suffered from the effects of his poor interpersonal relationships.

I suggested to the president that he consider a hypothetical situation. Suppose that the general manager decided to leave this job, only to come back in a few weeks wanting his old position back. "Knowing what you know about this person," I asked the president, "Would you rehire him into the same general manager position he had prior to his departure?" With no hesitation in his voice, the President responded, "Absolutely not!"

I then asked the president, "Aren't you rehiring him every day?" The president groaned upon realizing that he unconsciously supported poor performance by not holding the general manager accountable—and by "rehiring" him every day.

The "acid test" of determining whether a person continues to be good fit resides within the response to that key question: *"Would you rehire this person into the same position if this option were available?"* If your answer is *no,* then I have to challenge the advisability of keeping a person in the same position or even on the payroll. Sometimes the individual simply no longer fits with the current job requirements. Perhaps he has outgrown the job or the job has outgrown him! To keep one on the job under these circumstances serves neither the individual nor the organization.

Although I am not advocating wholesale dismissal of poor performers, I am advocating that you deal directly with performance issues in a way that simultaneously honors people. By being tough as nails on issues and tender with people, you can build a stronger spirit of accountability that benefits both The Bottom Line and The Human Element.

A chief executive of one of my client companies taught me a great way to respectfully terminate poor performers in a caring coaching context. It's direct, it's sensitive, and it gets results. Even labor attorneys see the benefits. This highly effective chief executive supports and values employees. He also recognizes that personnel changes are sometimes necessary. In a straightforward and sensitive manner, he introduces a coaching approach intended to avoid termination and sets the stage for parting company if significant performance improvements are not consistently achieved.

How does he do it? Three steps. The first two steps require intensive coaching and counseling as both the manager and the involved associate focus on clarification of performance expectations and delivering expected results. The third step results in separation.

1. *"I am* **beginning** *to lose confidence in your ability to* _____. *I want you to know that I support you, and I*

am on your team. Yet, your continued employment is contingent upon significant and consistent improvement in performance."

This coaching process reflects the tough and tender approach. Working together, the manager and associate identify critical performance strengths, stretches, and targets and develop specific performance improvement plans with appropriate timelines. The associate may need guidance in developing plans to assure that organizational needs are appropriately addressed. Provide the guidance, but don't spoon-feed the individual.

In the initial coaching session, set up at least two follow-up dates with the associate to both celebrate anticipated successes and take corrective action. The follow-up meetings apply creative pressure to consistently achieve performance expectations. If significant, positive, and consistent performance results are not achieved, advance to step two.

2. *"I am losing confidence in your ability to _____. I remain on your team and support your efforts to grow and develop. However, your continued employment is contingent upon significant and consistent improvement in performance."*

    Repeat the S-S-T coaching process emphasizing expected performance outcomes and time lines. Once again, build in follow-up sessions with specific meeting dates. If significant, positive, consistent improvement is not experienced, advance to step three.

3. *"I have lost confidence in your ability to _____. I continue to support your growth as a person. Nevertheless,*

at this point, we are having to part company." At
that point, you let the person go.

This clear, direct coaching process provides clarity of expectations and basically eliminates the "surprise element." Assertive, affirming communications are employed throughout the
process. Using the S-S-T coaching steps described earlier, the
associate develops specific action plans and goals related to performance. While building on strengths, this firm, yet fair approach clearly defines performance targets and specific action
steps required for achieving desired performance results.

The editors of *Positive Leadership* advocate a similar approach
they call a "Career Decision Day." When previous coaching efforts still have not produced the desired performance results,
engage the individual in making an accountable decision regarding her future employment. The time has come for a significant
choice to either do whatever it takes to produce the desired results or find employment elsewhere. On Friday, tell the employee
to take the following Monday off with pay and to use this time to
thoughtfully pursue one of two options:

1. Develop a S-S-T performance improvement plan
   intended to achieve significant and consistent
   results consistent with your expectations.
2. Prepare a letter of resignation for your
   acceptance.

If you feel that the individual cannot or will not perform
consistently with your bottom line and human element expectations, however, do not offer her the option of developing a performance improvement plan. Have the courage to instead release the employee to pursue other career options.

An appropriate termination provides an opportunity for
both the individual and the organization to create a brighter
future. Granted, termination is usually difficult for both parties.

Maintaining the individual in a poorly suited position, however, ultimately hurts both the individual and the organization. When you assist a person to seek career opportunities that better fit his talents and interests, he usually does better in the long run. Explore the following example that demonstrates this point:

> *Early in my consulting career, I had the difficult experience of having to "fire" one of my first major clients. This CEO of a large organization had lost support from his executive team, his board, and other key stakeholders. Yet, somehow, he continued to cling to his job, and the Board did not have the courage to terminate his services.*
>
> *Having just completed a series of interviews with his key stakeholders, I also concluded that he needed to leave. At that point, however, I had two major dilemmas: He was my first major client, and, because I was new in consulting and financially strapped at that time, "firing" my client presented an immediate, personal financial challenge.*
>
> *An "opportunity" presented itself to apply what I advocate. (It's always tougher to apply these principles to myself.) "Pausing" first, I explored what principles I needed to guide my decisions. I could not be pressured into making a decision to benefit my pocketbook. From an integrity perspective, the right thing to do became clear: The CEO needed to go. The question, then, became how to do that in a way that honored the "tough and tender" principle.*
>
> *Rather than hitting him with the highly critical findings from my just-completed stakeholder interviews, I elected to explore how he viewed his current job. Because "the answers are often within," I asked him what*

he liked most about his job as CEO. "Not much," he quietly responded. I then inquired how he felt about his job. He described how he frequently woke up at night worrying about how poorly things were going. In addition, he thought he was developing an ulcer. Finally, I asked how his wife felt about his job. "She hates it!" he responded. I noticed his slumped shoulders and avoidance of eye contact.

After letting him reflect on his own responses for a few moments, I asked him, "If you could be or do anything that you wanted from a career perspective, what would that be?" He looked up, thought for a while, then proceeded to describe his ideal job. When talking about that job, I noticed him sitting up in his chair, leaning forward toward me, talking faster and louder, and even having a bit of a smile on his face. Suddenly he stopped talking, looked directly at me and asked, "Do you think I should leave?"

Rather than giving him the answer, I asked him, "May I give you some feedback?" Having received his affirmative response, I shared my personal observations of his behavior when he described the current situation (his slumped shoulders, his slow speech, and his avoidance of eye contact). Then I shared my observations of the differences when he described his dream job (his looking up, his leaning forward, his more energetic voice, and his eye contact with me).

By assisting him to experience the contrast between his current and his dream job, he came to his own conclusions. "I need to leave!" he exclaimed with clarity and certainty. At that point, I simply asked, "Would you like to explore options about how you can leave that

will create a win for both you and the organization?"
"Yes!" he enthusiastically responded.

*After facilitating his decision-making process to
create a win-win outcome, he resigned to pursue a
job better suited to his talents and desires. Although I
effectively "fired" my client, the senior vice president
later became CEO and retained me to continue my
consulting relationship in building the new executive
team. (A win for me.) Eight years later, that former
CEO called to thank me for "encouraging him" to
pursue his dream job. He was healthy, happy, and
prosperous in his new job that more closely matched
his interests and talents.*

When things are not going well on the job, most (certainly
not all) people seem to recognize that they need to make significant changes. Their own fear may keep them, however, from
addressing those issues. By being firm, fair, and forthright, you
can facilitate others to discover what they need to address. By
drawing the answers out rather than putting them in, people are
more likely to experience a personal or professional wake-up
call. If individuals cannot or will not perform consistent with job
expectations, you have a distinct responsibility to provide them
with a "career opportunity elsewhere."

Building and sustaining great teams sometimes requires the
courage to make tough people-decisions. Obviously you need to
consider the cost of making a difficult decision—and the cost of
not making that decision. If one of your associates does not have
the aptitude or talent, does not have the right attitude, or is not
aligned with the corporate mission and values, you have a responsibility to make a change. You will discover that the long-
term cost of not making that decision will far exceed the short-
term costs. Have the courage to do the right thing.

"The ultimate measure of a man is not
where he stands in moments of comfort and convenience,
but where he stands at times of challenge and controversy."

—Martin Luther King, Jr.

---

career coaching:
linking individual with organizational interests

When leaders or coaches tap into the career purpose and passion of others, they ignite a spirit within that translates into great performance. Alignment of individual career interests with organizational needs facilitates the kind of match that brings out the best in people. Talents, interests, and career goals change, however, and require periodic assessment to sustain the passion of others in serving both your interests and theirs. For that reason, periodic exploration of **The 4 Career Guidance Questions** will result in a mutually beneficial outcome.

the 4 career guidance questions

Although most people agree that aligning corporate needs with individual talent is essential during an initial job interview, equal attention needs to be focused on ongoing career alignment as well. Because career interests change, periodic exploration of **The 4 Career Guidance Questions** with your key associates will assist in sustaining their long-term passion and commitment. Periodically explore with your key associates:

1. What makes work meaningful to you?

- What turns you **on** about work?
- What turns you **off** about work?

This question focuses on what motivates and de-motivates individuals while providing valuable insights about job fit and job assignments. When you discover the career passion of a person and link that to specific job assignments, your challenge will be holding them back from working too hard! When a person does what she loves, she never has to "work" again.

Having conducted coaching seminars for thousands of leaders, I frequently explore if any of those present have ever been asked by a boss, "What makes work meaningful to you, and how can I assist you experiencing even greater fulfillment while meeting the needs of the company?" This empowering question ignites the human spirit and releases purposeful creativity in delivering noteworthy results.

The small percentage of individuals fortunate enough to have had this experience report an increased sense of enthusiasm and elevated commitment to both their manager and their organization. Additionally, trust levels tend to increase as employees take more accountability for addressing their career development strategies while serving organizational interests.

By exploring individual career interests with your team, you may discover that what turns one person off about his job actually motivates another associate. Redirecting these work assignments may enable each to experience greater job fulfillment while simultaneously benefiting the organization.

When you discover the career interests of an associate and link those to current job assignments, you will likely release and empower your employees to perform at their best in delivering great results. Have the courage to explore their interests and to take creative action on their feedback.

2. If you had no limits, what would you be or do?

This question addresses the big-picture *dreams* of an individual and can provide useful insights about the experience that she is seeking. Armed with this information, current assignments might be modified to incorporate at least a portion of the person's interests in current assignments. By consciously seeking to create on the job at least some of what she is seeking in her dreams, professional fulfillment increases while simultaneously benefiting the organization.

In response to the "if you had no limits" question, a critical-care nurse manager in a large hospital said, "I would like to be an artist!" At first glance, her dream seemed entirely inconsistent with her present duties. In exploring the experience she sought, however, two specific ideas emerged that tapped into her interests while simultaneously serving the hospital.

The family waiting room adjacent to the Critical Care Unit was cold and institutional in appearance. By combining her nursing knowledge and artistic interests, she transformed the family waiting room into a warm, healing environment. Second, she created an informative critical-care family brochure, complete with her artwork. Both projects enabled her to use her artistic interests while serving the hospital needs. To her amazement, she learned to express her artistic interests within her existing job. The result? She generated greater job fulfillment while making an even greater contribution to the hospital—a win for both!

Discovering and pursuing your dream releases and empowers you to be your best, use your talents effectively, and experience greater career fulfillment. One individual, for example, identified backpacking as his career choice. How can one earn money backpacking? In pursuing this dream, he created a great job field-testing backpacking equipment for a large sporting goods manufacturing company. An entrepreneurial woman in my community loves to shop. How can one make money shopping? She developed an executive shopping service. She has her "black belt" in shopping and saves her busy clients time and energy while generating income shopping for them.

Letting go of your limits and creatively pursuing your interests can generate a win-win outcome. If you had no limits, what would you do?

_____

> "To understand the heart and mind of a person,
> look not at what he has already achieved,
> but at what he aspires to."
>
> —Kahlil Gibran

_____

3. What would cause you to:

A. Join a particular company?

B. Leave a company?

This key question reveals the core values that drive an associate's career decisions and reveals strategies that can be applied in empowering that individual. People join a company for such diverse reasons as career advancement, nature of work, opportunity to use their talents, status, compensation, location, and scheduling flexibility. Others prioritize compensation and benefits, reputation, short- or long-term term financial interests, job security, and organizational mission. By listening to their responses, you can gain great insights about how to align their interests with company needs.

The second part of this question provides understanding about what would cause an employee to leave. Listen for such concerns as limited career opportunities, lack of challenging work, having an insensitive boss, poor working conditions, or a work culture poorly matched with the associate's values. Knowing their career interests and task preferences provides an opportunity to assure a great job fit, make meaningful job assignments, and enhance job fulfillment.

4. To experience an even more fulfilling career:

A. What can I do as your manager?

B. What can you do?

This last question builds accountability into the empowerment process while clarifying mutual expectations. Both the manager and the employee share responsibility to explore and discover what empowerment strategies work best for the individual while simultaneously serving the organization. Having an open, safe discussion will reveal tangible action items that can be implemented by both the manager and associate in bringing about mutually beneficial results.

Effective empowerment begins with discovering what motivates people and matching those unique interests to the needs of the organization. Developing and releasing individual interests in service to both the associate and the organization expands the ROI of human capital while building commitment, supporting creativity, and enhancing productivity. Once you have the right people in the right job, you are now positioned to release human potential through effective coaching.

As a coach, your job is to develop the talent of your associates by providing them with clarity of direction, encouraging them to use their "gifts" effectively, building their confidence, and enhancing their competence. Effective coaching requires that *you* also commit to personal and professional development. Role-modeling self-development, as you develop others, raises the bar for achieving even greater results.

"If you want to be successful, it's just this simple:
Know what you are doing,
love what you are doing,
and believe in what you are doing.
It's just that simple."

—Will Rogers

---

retain your own coach!

One of my clients impressed upon me the value of ongoing growth and development. Perhaps this story will have a similar impact on you.

Steve Clifford, president of National Mobile Television, retained me to work with this leadership team to enhance individual, team, and organizational results in what was an already-effective company. At the conclusion of the first of a three-day leadership development and planning workshop, he and I met to explore plans for the following two days. I carefully outlined my content and process intended to achieve his outcomes. After reviewing my action steps for the remainder of the workshop, he looked me in the eye and asked, "Is that the best you can do?"

"Is that the best you can do?!" Never had a client asked me that question. My defensiveness peaked as I silently recited my resume of accomplishments as a former top executive and now a seasoned international consultant having worked with the best organizations. I couldn't believe the audacity of his question.

At that point, I finally paused and reconsidered his question. What a great question! "Is that the best you can do?" Why am I not always asking myself that question? He challenged me to be my best in service to his company—and he had every right to expect my best.

I then looked him in the eye and said, "I would like to have breakfast with you tomorrow morning before the session starts, and I will answer your question then."

In my hotel room that night, I tore the seminar apart. I reexamined his outcomes and expectations. I tested my approach, my strategies, and my content to assure that they served the client at the highest level. I prepared myself as never before for a meeting with a chief executive officer.

At breakfast the next morning, I again looked Steve in the eye and confidently said, "Yes. That is the best I can do!" His response startled me, "Good. That's all I wanted to know!"

That CEO challenged me to be and give my best. What a powerful and important lesson! What if everybody in your company challenged themselves with the question: "Is that the best I can do?" And, what if you continually challenged yourself with that same question? In the long run, both you and the organization win. Consciously doing your best results in Deliberate Success. Thanks for the great lesson, Steve.

Are you focused on developing your personal and professional best? Do you have a developmental plan, and are you working that plan? Who are you seeking out to develop your "gifted" areas? What have you learned in the past year to increase your value? What untapped potential do you see in yourself? Not only is it important for you to be a coach, but it is likewise important that you actively seek coaches to develop your personal and professional best.

Tiger Woods, identified as the finest golfer in history, consistently drives the ball 330 yards straight down the fairway. His physical form is perfect. His mental game is positive and focused. His results are awesome! He has mastered his craft, yet he keeps getting better. And he has a golf coach.

Harvey Mackay, author of several best-sellers, including *Swim With The Sharks Without Being Eaten Alive, Dig Your Well Before You Are Thirsty,* and *Pushing The Envelope,* earns top dollar as a keynote speaker. Toastmaster's International selected Mackay as one of the five best presenters in the world. He has mastered his keynote presentations. And he has a speech coach.

I think there is a message here! Why do people who are already doing exceptionally well have coaches? They have committed to that challenging process of lifelong learning and personal mastery. They consciously seek to reinvent themselves. They don't settle for what they have already mastered; they commit to stretching themselves to higher and more refined levels of performance. They also seek the learning opportunities provided by outside resources: coaches who observe, encourage, and push the envelope.

"Your imagination is your preview of life's coming attractions."

—Denis Waitley

I have been a coach and mentor to executives throughout the country as they seek to enhance their personal and professional effectiveness. These people are strong enough to be vulnerable—vulnerable to seek outside feedback that both challenges and encourages. They have the courage to actively seek external assessments and experiment with new ways of enhancing both their business practices and their personal lives.

Addressing your own personal and professional issues has to be the toughest work that one can do in life. Yet this growth process can stimulate quantum-leap growth spurts to higher levels of personal and professional fulfillment.

I consistently find that peak performers in all career fields are far more willing to retain coaches than are the second stringers. Like the Japanese practice of Kaizen, these peak performers seek constant, incremental improvement. To be

deliberate success gem

Teaching: The Business Success Delivery System

Contributed by Jeffrey Israel, M.D.

Ongoing success of a business requires a conscious commitment to teaching, coaching, and learning—for you and your associates. Teaching of people is the Business Success Delivery System, especially when the development methods engage your associates in the heart and soul of sound principles and practices of entrepreneurship, private enterprise, and personal and financial achievement.

Many people who want to start out on their own are held back due to fear and lack of knowledge. Perhaps their fear stems out of never having been guided. How would business—indeed life—be different if one had a personal mentor to teach, share, and empower an attitude of Deliberate Success? Imagine having a coach equivalent to the Tiger Woods of business strategy and learning from him how to hit the long drives, the short chips, and the one-putting of each green for one's business future. Having experts to guide you can make a significant difference in the business success you achieve.

(cont.)

of high value, they must commit to life-long learning. Rather than seeking mastery, they come *from* a place of mastery. Learning, growing, stretching, and experimenting is a way of life for those who practice personal mastery. And so is the investment in having a coach.

Do I have a coach? You bet. Several, in fact: a media coach, a speech coach, and a few consulting coaches. I am consciously reinventing each part of my consulting practice both to benefit to my clients and to experience greater professional fulfillment. My top executive clients are rightfully demanding and expecting the best from me. As an advocate of coaching, I have a responsibility to apply the same principle to myself.

I also meet with two "growth partners" each month. As trusted friends, we commit to telling our truth and to coaching one another. Part of our agreement is to practice the "tough and tender" principle. Each of us benefits from hearing the insights and observations of the others as we deal with our life issues. Speaking our truth and hearing the truth of others is risky business. Yet, I have learned that not doing so is an even greater risk.

Have the courage to invest in a coach. Seek out one who will

(cont. from p. 228) Effectively linking your associates with a network of successful men and women committed to teaching and sharing knowledge will produce long-term, positive business results. A flexible, uniquely designed plan that honors individual dreams and interests while serving the business produces win-win outcomes for sustained success.

Ongoing education means going to school—the school of life. Because our teachers come in many forms, be prepared to fully engage in the study of audiotapes of people's success stories, in reading from books by the likes of Napoleon Hill and Dale Carnegie, and attending training sessions that teach principles of success. By harnessing new ideas and enhancing personal growth, you and your associates will prosper while experiencing an even more fulfilling life journey.

—Jeffrey M. Israel, M.D.
Quixtar Diamond
Independent Business Owner
www.quixtar.com
jisrael@quixnet.net

hold your feet to the fire and give you candid, quality feedback— the kind of feedback that is tough on issues. Be bold in soliciting feedback about what is going well and what requires attention. Listen with every bone in your body to the feedback, for there may be a valuable gem buried in the data. As a wise cowboy once said, *"With all this manure around here, there's got to be a pony somewhere!"*

Feedback is a gift, and an experienced coach can provide you with insights that enable you to draw the very best from your personal talent pool. By finely honing your talent to optimum levels of performance, your increased value will ultimately result in higher levels of compensation, will open career doors, and will provide you with a personal sense of fulfillment that ignites your passion. Renewing and reinventing yourself positions you for Deliberate Success.

"It's a funny thing about life;
if you refuse to accept anything but the best,
you very often get it."

—Somerset Maughan

---

deliberate success
strategy 5: renewal

sustaining your competitive edge

"Even if you're on the right track,
you will get run over if you just sit there."

—Will Rogers

chapter 13

the "3r's" of renewal:

release, reaffirm, reinvent

> "As our case is new, we must think and act anew."
>
> —**Abraham Lincoln**

MAINTAINING THE STATUS quo in a competitive environment is not a viable option. Dinosaurs tried this tactic, and it didn't work. Similarly, if *you* merely stayed at your current state of development for the next several years, you might become an "endangered species" in your own profession. Ask yourself, "Am I lagging behind in my field, am I just keeping up, or am I one of the progressive leaders?" Even if you are moving ahead, the speed you are moving must be faster than the speed global business advances—otherwise, you will still be trailing behind! Rather than being concerned about *employment*, you need to focus instead on your *employability*. Any way you look at it, you need to reinvent yourself at a fairly good clip.

> "If you do not deal with significant issues of the past,
> the past will catch up and deal with you"
>
> —Eric Allenbaugh

Futurists estimate that 50 percent of the jobs that will be available in the next 10 years have not even been invented yet. To sustain your competitive edge and assure your employability, you must commit to a continual process of reinventing yourself—or suffer the consequences of obsolescence and extinction. Change comes with the territory, and adaptable, learning individuals and organizations will clearly prevail over those that have fallen in love with their current status. Tom Peters succinctly communicates this message in his typically provocative way: "Somebody is going to do you in. The only question: Who will it be? A competitor—or you?"

Deliberate Success—getting from where you are now to where you want or, perhaps, *need* to be—requires a conscious process of working through the "3 R's" of renewal:

1. **Release**: What must you *release* or let go of to provide room and resources to support your growth? Consider, for example, releasing obsolete products and services, negative behaviors and attitudes, limiting beliefs, unhealthy relationships, and bureaucratic policies and practices.

2. **Reaffirm:** What existing strengths and resources do you need to *reaffirm* and intensify to support your next growth steps? Consider, for example, reaffirming your commitment to stellar customer service, empowering employees, lifelong learning, and fiscal viability.

3. **Reinvent:** How might you *reinvent* yourself to assure that you are at the cutting edge in your field

the "3 Rs" of renewal:
Release, Reaffirm, and Reinvent

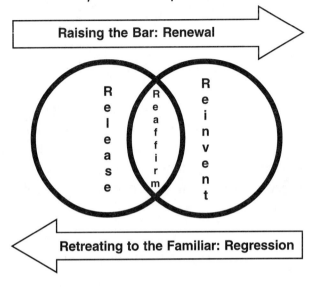

while simultaneously contributing to your career fulfillment? Consider, for example, reinventing your products and services, delighting your customers, expanding your knowledge, increasing your value, building new skills, and developing new markets.

"When you're not learning—someone, somewhere else, is. When you meet—guess who has the advantage?"

—Bob Pritchard

The "3 R's" apply equally to both individual and organizational renewal. Recall years ago when the computer field identified IBM as the benchmark of the industry. It was on top. When purchasing computer equipment, people typically asked: "Is this IBM-compatible?" You don't hear that question anymore. Why? IBM fell in love with its way of doing business, fell in love with mainframe computers, and fell in love with promoting top leaders exclusively from within. It could not adapt and let go of some of its culture that no longer served it well in the current business environment.

IBM became an "endangered species" in the 1980s as it lost significant market share to its more adaptive competitors that provided cutting-edge hardware, software, and services to its customers. Market conditions forced IBM to take drastic action—massive layoffs. At the brink of extinction, its corporate "wake-up call" finally mobilized IBM into action. Having learned a difficult lesson, IBM returned to greatness by deliberately reinventing itself.

"The problem is never how to get new, innovative thoughts into your mind, but how to get old ones out."

—Dee Hock, Founder and former CEO, Visa

In contrast, Jack Welch, who headed General Electric during its transformational period from 1980 through 2001, clearly understood the "3 R's." Described as one of the world's most fabled CEOs, Welch deliberately released some old ways of doing business that no longer served GE. He strongly and consistently reaffirmed basic business values, yet reinvented GE through and through. Under his leadership, GE transformed from manufacturing household appliances to becoming a highly adaptive, diverse global business producing aircraft engines, providing financial services, and even expanding into television production.

Welch demonstrated a compulsive commitment to assuring that the GE mission and values transcended his own leadership. An internally driven succession-planning process of six years ultimately resulted in the careful selection of Jeffrey Immelt as his successor. If that were not enough, Welch implemented a nearly one-year overlap and coaching process to assure an effective handoff to Immelt.

According to the November 28, 2000 issue of The Oregonian, when Welch announced his successor in late 2000, he made it clear: "It's all going to unfold very nicely—you won't see a bump." Immelt, his newly appointed successor then said, "I have a tremendous passion for the company. We simply have the best team in the world." Success is not an accident. Even as Welch released his leadership at GE, he reinforced the principles that made it great and positioned the new leader to be successful. It's no wonder Fortune magazine describes GE as "the most admired company in the world."

"For something new to begin, something must end."

—Kris King

Tiger Woods isn't just a great athlete; he dominates the field of great golfers. Sure, he came into this world gifted with unusual abilities. Yet he finely hones those natural abilities with a commitment to reinventing himself—daily! Here's what other athletes had to say about Tiger in the June 18, 2001, issue of *Newsweek*: *"Tiger works harder than anyone out there, and that's why he's kicking butt,"* said tennis great Martina Navratilova, winner of 167 singles titles. *"No matter who you are, no matter how good an athlete you are, we're creatures of habit,"* reported hockey legend Wayne Gretzky. *"The better your habits are, the better they'll be in pressure situations."* Gretzky went on to say that *"When I watch golf and hear other players interviewed, most of them sound like they can't believe they won. Then you hear from Tiger, and he either expected to win or can't believe he didn't. It's a different mind-set altogether."*

"Successful people do what unsuccessful people are unwilling to do."

—Zig Zigler

Tiger Woods and other great athletes don't leave success up to chance. They deliberately delete that which does not serve them well, they work at developing their intrinsic talent, and they push the envelop to create even higher levels of performance. Great athletes and great leaders commit to practicing the "3 Rs" as a conscious, deliberate commitment to success. Ken Blanchard and Michael O'Connor encourage you to take a hard look at the quality of your life journey as you create what you seek in life in the following section.

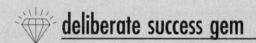 **deliberate success gem**

Managing by Values: the "Acts" of Life

Contributed by Kenneth Blanchard, Ph.D.
and Michael O'Connor, Ph.D.

We have experienced an increasing number of executives who appear outwardly successful but who are actually inwardly unhappy and unfulfilled. They may appear to have it all together, but they really feel empty inside. This discovery of emptiness is painful, but it can also be a very good sign, a "wake-up call" that drives a person to see where they are, to see where they want to be, and to chose a course of action that works even better for them and for the lives they touch.

Three acts in life shape who we are, what we learn, what we contribute, and, ultimately, what levels of satisfaction and fulfillment we experience:

- **Act I:**   Achieve
- **Act II:**   Connect
- **Act III:**   Integrate

Act I is to **Achieve**. Achieving is a natural act for human beings. The only problem is that many people think that Achieve is the only act in town. They're always looking for the next victory, the next sale, or the next conquest. But you know what? I've never heard of anyone on their deathbed who said, "I wish I'd gone to the office more."

Act II, **Connect**, is about relationships. Sometimes it takes a personal crisis, such as financial strife, lack of success in one's career, or physical illness, to make a person see that what really matters in his or her life is people. Remember the classic turnaround old Scrooge made. He went from being a lonely grump to a man beloved by all—in a single night! Act II involves being generous with your time and talents and demonstrating a genuine interest in friends, family, and others.

Act III, **Integrate**, means bringing it all together in a way that provides personal meaning in our lives. Here you must first define, or redefine, your own purpose and values, and then put them into daily action in ways that are truly meaningful to you. It may be time to ask yourself: *What is my purpose? Has my life been about following my dream, or has it been about following somebody else's dream? Or, has everything up to now been a preparation for what I've really come to do?*

Whether on a personal or organizational level, these questions must be answered. Defining your purpose isn't just an intellectual process of arriving at a logical conclusion. You have to dig deeper, to the level of your inner values. What are the core values that, for you or your organization, will guide and shape the way you fulfill your purpose? After you've identified these values, the toughest question follows: How are we demonstrating these values in our everyday dealings with the world?

In times of constant change, it's easy for people to think that even the fundamental laws governing human responses and interactions have changed. But they haven't. The same kinds of basic considerations required now have always been needed to keep employees committed, customers delighted, stockholders satisfied, and suppliers and creditors glad to do business with you.

How we perform in each of the three acts determines the quality of our life journey, the results we attain in our organization, and even what kind of a world we are cocreating. Create, in your personal life, in your organization, and in your world the quality of performance deserving of a standing ovation for each act!

—Kenneth Blanchard, Ph.D.
Coauthor of *The One-Minute Manager,*
Managing by Values,
and *Leadership By The Book*
www.blanchardlearning.com

—Michael O'Connor, Ph.D.
Coauthor of *The Platinum Rule*
and *Managing By Values*

focus on increasing your value

The most valuable career development advice I have ever been given came from Dr. Don Murray, a friend and fellow consultant. While in my early years of consulting, Don said to me, "Whenever you have contact with a client, make sure you provide them with something of value—an idea, a solution, an article. They will then associate you with value." Imagine the many doors that open to you when people associate you with providing value? (In contrast, many employees consume organizational resources—you don't want to be in that camp!) To assure that you are providing present value and positioning yourself for future value, consciously seek to reinvent yourself, learn new ways, engage in cutting-edge activities, and let go of old baggage.

> "Learning is not compulsory—neither is survival."
>
> **—W. Edwards Deming**

As president of your own Personal Services Corporation, according to Brian Tracy, you have a distinct responsibility to provide high value to your client (your employer) by continually reinventing yourself. Instead of waiting for your company to provide continuing education, pay for it yourself. (You are worth the investment.) Instead of asking for more money, ask for more responsibility. Instead of looking at how much money you are earning, look at how much value you are providing. Instead of seeking to avoid assignments, volunteer for activities that benefit the organization. When you consistently provide high value to your employer, you will, in the long run, expand your influence, achieve greater results, and even generate significantly higher income.

> "I couldn't wait for success—so I went ahead without it."
>
> **—Jonathan Winters**

What specific, tangible steps are you now taking to increase your value in this global economy? What talents do you offer and what benefits do you provide that will encourage both employers and customers to continue to knock at your door? What deliberate action steps are you taking to release that which no longer serves you, to reaffirm and enhance your intrinsic talents, and to reinvent yourself to provide even higher value in the future?

> "It is not the strongest species that survive,
> nor the most intelligent,
> but the ones most responsive to change."
>
> —Charles Darwin

chapter 14

individual renewal

be what you seek!

*"A musician must make music,
an artist must paint,
a poet must write
if he is to be ultimately at peace with himself.
What one can be, one must be."*

—Abraham Maslow

the "4 d's" of deliberate success

DELIBERATE SUCCESS, IN business and in life, starts with a *dream.* You cannot experience the reality of a dream without having first dreamed the dream! Nothing is more powerful than a compelling vision that ignites your spirit, touches your soul, and sharpens your competitive edge.

Next, you need to *decide* that this dream is important enough to pursue. Most of what you want in life is just a decision away. You need to say yes to your dream, or it will never happen. At the same time, you need to say no to those other activities that detract from your dream. Pay attention to what you say yes to and what you say no to in business and in life. The answers reveal your values, and your priorities—and eventually determine your outcomes.

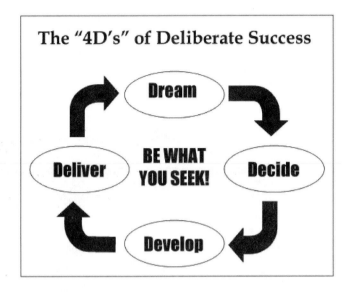

After deciding to move ahead with your dream, your next step is to *develop* the action plans that will get you from where you are now to where you want to be. In this phase, imagine that you are already where you want to be: what does that desired state look like, sound like, and feel like? Allowing yourself to fully experience the desired state provides greater clarity in determining what action steps will be required to achieve your results. You will benefit from first identifying major themes or strategies to get from your current to your desired state. Each strategy can then be broken down into specific action steps which clearly identify who is going to do what by when.

The final step, *deliver,* requires that you have the courage to act on your plan. Those who achieve Deliberate Success punch through barrier after barrier. Second-string people, on the other hand, seem to seek security at the key choice points and merely retreat to that which is familiar to them. They ultimately repeat the same patterns of behavior that keep them in a perpetual "stuck state cycle." You, however, recognize that commitment to a dream, coupled with the courage to act, results in Deliberate

Success. You become a "personal delivery system" to manifest your dream.

"The future does not get better by hope—it gets better by plan."

—Jim Rohn

I applied the "4 D's" to a personal career change more than two decades ago and have further developed that dream after these many years. Although I enjoyed my then-career in hospital administration, I had a *dream* to start my own consulting business. As my dream continued to grow, it eventually captured my spirit. So what was that compelling dream? *"By assisting individuals and organizations to create and sustain their best and by giving more to life than I receive, I will experience a high degree of personal and professional fulfillment and will achieve financial independence."* At one point, I made a *decision* to act on the dream. That decision set into motion what ultimately became a new and even more fulfilling career. I left my hospital position on a Friday and started my doctoral program and consulting practice on the following Monday. It was scary and exciting stuff!

"The path to success is to take massive, determined action."

—Anthony Robbins

To achieve the results I sought, I needed to *develop* a plan to get me form hospital administration to a high level of performance in the consulting field. My plan included:

1. A clear and compelling vision.
2. Three major strategies to pursue in getting to where I wanted to be.

3. Specific action items within each of the three strategies to catapult me forward.

Finally, I needed the courage to *deliver,* to put my plan into action in spite of the many obstacles that I needed to punch through. That decision set into motion what ultimately became a new and even more fulfilling career. I left my hospital position on a Friday and started my doctoral program and consulting practice on the following Monday. It was scary, yet exciting!

If you still lack clarity of purpose or have not yet experienced that internal driving force for Deliberate Success, then carefully explore the following **15 Key Life Planning Questions** to discover your passion.

 deliberate success gem

Moving Past Objections

Contributed by Richard Thalheimer

Most good ideas are not immediately received by other people. For some, a new idea becomes a problem in itself. People are used to doing things their way, and new ideas tend to upset the situation. If all objections must be overcome first, nothing will ever succeed!

Satisfying everyone's objections will keep any project from even getting started. At some point, it is better to simply launch the new project, even though all the loose ends are not completely tied up.

It's better to have a project started with a chance of success in the future than never launch the project at all. Yet, most projects are never even attempted, because there are too many objections to overcome.

Sort through your ideas. Boil them down to the one you want to pursue. And then get started—despite the objections!

—Richard Thalheimer
Chairman & Founder, The Sharper Image
www.sharperimage.com

This process may well be a life-changing experience for you, as it has for so many of my executive clients.

"The best way to predict your future is to create it."

—Stephen Covey

---

the 15 key life planning questions

You are already familiar with the two primary motivators in coaching others: doing something that makes you feel good about yourself and doing something that makes a difference. Now it's time to apply these to yourself. Discovering your passion energizes, enlightens, and enlivens your life experience. The following exercise will make a significant difference in your life, so give your very best to discovering and developing your life's passion. What better time than now to clarify and live your life's purpose?

Identify the most creative part of your day to work through this self-discovery process. I encourage you to write out your responses to these questions, for writing engages both the logical and creative parts of your brain. Be willing to let your creative energy flow, and consciously resist that part of you that may want to put limits on your own development. In this important exercise, you want to be fully present!

Let the following questions guide your inner wisdom, the part of you that knows. Let your pen explore ideas you have only dreamed about in the past as you create new insights, new clarity, and new direction. Be willing to experiment, venture into new territory, and discover the learning. **The 15 Key Life Planning Questions** will open up a new adventure in your life. Enjoy the discovery.

1. **TALENTS:** What are your most significant and unique talents and gifts that you bring to the organization and to life? List no less than seven. (The question here is *not* "How smart am I?" Instead, ask "*How* am I smart?")
2. **INTERESTS:** What do you like to do most? What gets your creative juices flowing?
3. **ENERGY DRAINS:** What do you like to do least? What turns you off?
4. **DREAMS:** If you had no limits, what would you be, do, and have?
5. **"GOING TO" VALUES:** If you were going to join a particular company, what would you look for in that company that would light your fire?
6. **"MOVING AWAY FROM" VALUES:** What would cause you to leave a particular company?
7. **WAKE-UP CALLS:** If you were told by a physician that you were likely to suddenly die within one year, what would you do differently with your life in the remaining time?
8. **FINANCIAL FREEDOM:** If you were to win a multimillion dollar lottery, what would you do differently in your career and in your lifestyle?
9. **ALIGNMENT:** Think about times in your life when you were working hard, yet experiencing great fulfillment. What were you doing? Describe your actions and feelings.
10. **BALANCE:** Think about times in your life that you were playing and thoroughly enjoying yourself. What were you doing?
11. **AVOCATION:** Bring to mind your most pleasurable hobbies or interests. What are they and how might you incorporate these into a new career, your

existing career, or to simply create more of this experience in your life?

12. **CHILDLIKE PERSPECTIVE:** Imagine that you are now 8 years old and looking ahead at your life with all the imagination and confidence of a child. What dreams do you want to fulfill?

13. **SAGE WISDOM:** Imagine that you are now 80 years old and looking back over your life with the wisdom and insight of a sage elder. What pleases you most about your accomplishments? What do you regret not having done?

14. **CIRCLE OF INFLUENCE:** Imagine that the most highly respected people you know are having a conversation about you. What positive things would you want them to be saying about your principles, your values, and your contributions?

15. **PASSAGES:** Imagine that your life came to a close, and people gathered to celebrate your life. What would you like them to be saying in your obituary about you as a person and about the difference you made in this world?

---

*"If you want to know your future,
look at what you are doing in this moment."*

—Ancient Tibetan Teaching

After several days of reflection time, return to refine your written responses where appropriate. Begin to look for common themes in the responses. You are now operating in a diamond field of priceless ideas that will make a long-term difference.

Your dreams are usually only a decision away. After you have refined your responses, ask yourself the following questions about the new clarity you have achieved through this "Discovering Your Life's Passion" exercise:

1. What *major challenges* must I overcome to manifest this dream?
2. What old ways, behaviors, and non-productive attitudes do I need to *release* to make room for this dream?
3. What major *costs* would I experience if I elected *not* to pursue this dream?
4. What major *benefits* will I experience as a result of manifesting this dream?
5. What *action steps* do I intend to take now that will bring me closer to realizing my dream?

"You can show up in life any way you want to.
You just have to decide how you want to show up."

—Karen Sheridan

---

creating your personal mission statement

You are now positioned to take the next step in creating your personal, written Mission Statement (What is my purpose?) and your Vision Statement (Where am I going?). Like organizational mission and vision statements, this will serve as your "Navigational Guide" in creating what you are seeking in life.

In my own family, we created a combined Mission and Vision Statement that continues to have a profound influence in our ways of both "being" and "doing." (It's tough being married to a consultant—we actually do these things!) We periodically set aside a weekend for our own renewal and use this time to review our Family Mission and Vision Statement, celebrate successes, and take whatever action will enable us to fulfill the spirit of this family commitment. This not only assists in keeping our relationship current and vibrant, it provides clarity of what we want to cocreate in our world. Implementation of our family's mission and vision statement, additionally, has had a profoundly positive impact on the quality of our relationship and in our life fulfillment.

I am sharing Our Family Mission and Vision Statement, not to impose my values on you, but to serve as a

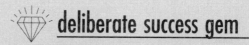

deliberate success gem

Facilitating Revolutionary Change

Contributed by Ron Allen

Facing up to the need for fundamental or revolutionary change is daunting for any person or organization. Expectations are turned upside down. Lives are disrupted. There are fear and deep concern about the future. In today's world, however, change on a vast scale often is absolutely necessary. We faced that need at Delta Air Lines, and we've taken steps to gain control of our future. I'm new to this business of revolutionary change, but I have learned three lessons that might be useful.

First, your idea for change must be clear and compelling. People will join you when they understand that change is necessary and that the results are worth the extraordinary effort needed. It's up to the leader to articulate that idea and communicate constantly to remind people of the reason and the result. Change starts at the top.

Second, change must be fast and constant. Speed counts. Expect more of yourself and your people, and expect it faster than either you or they think is possible. People have vast reservoirs of talent and energy that can be tapped when they understand what is expected of them and make a commitment to get the job done. **(cont.)**

(cont. from p. 251) Not everyone will come along at the same pace, but people will surprise you. Let them.

And, third, don't be intimidated by the doubts and the doubters. Revolutionary change is hard work. There are contradictions and no easy decisions. Others will second-guess every step you take. You'll make mistakes, and so will others. A sure conviction that the course you are on is absolutely necessary and correct will keep the doubts and doubters at bay. Commitment is contagious.

The reward comes when the change takes hold and momentum turns in the right direction.

—Ronald W. Allen
Former Chairman, President, and CEO,
Delta Air Lines, Inc.
www.delta.com

sample for you to create a personal mission and vision statement that honors your interests, values, and life goals:

our family mission and vision statement

With God at the center of our lives and home, our family purpose is to create a nurturing, safe environment that:

- honors individual differences,
- creates giants out of self and others,
- encourages spiritual, emotional and physical development,
- role models loving relationships,
- promotes caring, open communications, and
- *makes a positive, joyful difference in our inner and outer worlds.*

—Eric and Kay Allenbaugh

★★★

Whether by design or by default, you are shaping your future. Robert Allen, a financial expert and speaker, describes your purpose as the intersection of four key elements:

1. Your talents.
2. Your interests.

3. Your values
4. Your intuition.

When you align these four elements with clarity, the magic of your life's purpose begins to unfold.

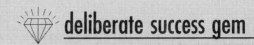 **deliberate success gem**

Mastering Your Own
Personal Services Corporation

Contributed by Brian Tracy

You are the president of your own Personal Services Corporation—the Chief Executive Officer of your own life. You are responsible for your own personal business. You are in charge of production, distribution, marketing, quality, finance, and research and development. You even determine your own salary.

As the president of your own Personal Services Corporation, everything that affects business in the world today affects your personal business as well. Every innovation, discovery, and paradigm shift in business is as applicable to you as a person as it is to a multibillion dollar corporation. The men and women who will survive and thrive in the years ahead are those who are continually looking around for ideas and insights that they can use to be faster, more flexible, and more effective in their work on a day-to-day basis.

Companies and individuals that have clear, written values and mission statements based on those values are more profitable and successful than those that do not. You can dramatically improve the quality of your life by identifying your core values and committing yourself to live consistently by those values, no matter what the external circumstances may be. Once you determine what your personal values are, you can organize your life around them. Values give you a basis or a foundation upon which you can make your decisions.

Imagine that the film crew of *60 Minutes* is going to come into your community and do a story on you. They are going to ask all the people who know you what kind of a person you are, what sort of values you have, and what you stand for as an individual. They will explore your philosophy and beliefs, based on your words and actions.

What would the *60 Minutes* profile demonstrate about your "Personal Services Corporation?" What would the people around you say about your past and present? What behavioral observations would they report about your mission, vision, and values? What would they say about your performance, your quality, and your adaptability to changing market conditions? What would they say about your future?

Successful companies invariably sit down and think through the answers to these questions. Dr. Theodore Leavitt of the Harvard Business School says that a company's reputation is its most valuable asset in the marketplace. Its products, processes, and people may all change over time, but its reputation can last for decades. It is the same with you. What kind of reputation do you have in your marketplace? And what kind of reputation would you like to create for yourself in the future?

Sit down and write out your core values and mission statement. These become your operating principles and identify who you are and who you commit to become. When you begin to see yourself as an active participant in the dynamic world around you, you take full control of your own destiny. And your future becomes unlimited.

—Brian Tracy
President, Brian Tracy International
www.briantracy.com

> *"I am still learning."*
>
> **—Michelangelo**

Renewal starts with having the courage to take a look at your own life and to boldly explore where you are now, where you want to be, and how you can close the gap. This self-examination process builds on strengths, clarifies individual growth targets, and identifies stretches (actions needed for renewal and reinventing). Deliberate Success requires that you periodically reinvent yourself to assure that you are achieving your important goals and experiencing maximum personal and professional fulfillment. This cannot be left up to chance; reinvention requires deliberate planning and follow-through.

By discovering, developing, and directing your gifted area or talent, you can experience making a positive—even joyful—difference in both your inner and outer worlds. Inside, you experience enhanced self worth and greater life fulfillment. What you attract from the outside reflects what is going on inside.

Being "on purpose" requires a conscious commitment to living your dream, your principles, and your values on a daily basis. You have three ways to convert your dream into reality: making a series of small, incremental changes that inch you toward your dream; taking quantum-leap action steps that propel you quickly toward your dream; or coming *from* what you are seeking. Although each strategy works, coming *from* want you want engages your spirit and enables you to achieve your desired outcomes with greater speed and passion.

To assure that you are "on purpose" at the choice points in your life, pause and ask yourself these questions:

1. **Are my thoughts and actions in alignment with my purpose, passion, and values?**

2. **Is what I am doing right now bringing me closer to or farther from the realization of my dream?**

3. **Am I coming *from* that place of being "on purpose?"**

Don't put off identifying and doing your dream; *be* what you seek! Be your dream. Be your goals. Rather than *seeking* success, *bring* success to what you want to be and do through conscious, deliberate actions. You are the architect of your future, and you know how to make it happen. Trust yourself to apply that which you already know and use your gifts wisely in service to yourself, to your employer, and to making a positive difference in our world.

"Twenty years from now, you will be more disappointed
by the things you didn't do than by the ones you did.
So throw off the bowlines. Sail away from the safe harbor.
Catch the tradewinds in your sails. Explore. Dream. Discover."

—Mark Twain

chapter 15

organizational renewal

deliver cutting-edge results

> "Look into the future and ask: What is the future going to look like?
> What can I do to be in the right spot at the right time?
> Once it's obvious to everyone that something is going to be successful,
> the opportunity is gone. Then anybody can do it!"
>
> **—Ted Turner**

RAPIDLY CHANGING TECHNOLOGY, rising consumer expectations, and global competition require that you reinvent your products and services faster and more effectively than does your competition. Corporate graveyards are full of organizations that have failed to keep pace with exponential change. The Polaroid Corporation dominated the field of instant photography for decades, yet basically ignored the emerging technology of digital cameras. Producing even better chemical cameras was not the solution; its customers wanted computer compatible cameras. Polaroid paid a big price for not reinventing itself.

Although the organizational mission remains relatively constant over the years, vision periodically changes. Leaders must constantly renew themselves, their organization, and their products and services to assure they are competitive, current, and relevant.

Organizations that sustain long-term success balance principle-centered, value-driven basics with the ability to adapt; this can be thought of as "roots and wings." Not for a moment do they forget their roots regarding the three core fundamentals of mission, vision, and culture. These qualities made them great and will continue to sustain their greatness. Leaders test every decision and action against their "roots" to assure ongoing alignment with the basics.

Astute leaders simultaneously and passionately function as change agents to position individuals, teams, products, and services to function at the cutting edge in meeting the needs of customers. People are empowered to function at their creative best to soar with the eagles—to spread their "wings." Leaders having a long-term track record of Deliberate Success intuitively understand the significant benefits of honoring both their roots (being grounded in principles) and their wings (applying their talent for maximum benefit).

In referring to the following diagram titled "Sustaining Deliberate Success," note **The 3 Key Leadership Principles**, **The 6 Core Leadership Strategies**, and **The Power of "And."** Wise leaders build each of these components into the planning process and operational application to assure lasting and positive results.

This Deliberate Success Action Model provides a blueprint for leaders to focus renewal efforts on the key elements that sustain impressive results. Moving from left to right, the **3 Key Leadership Principles** (Mission, Vision, and Culture) provide the foundation for any planning and operational activities. The **6 Core Leadership Strategies** focus on key factors to assure Deliberate Success. The **Power of "And"** reinforces outcomes sought on both The Bottom Line *and* The Human Element. Feedback from these results link into the **"3 R's of Renewal: Release, Reaffirm, and**

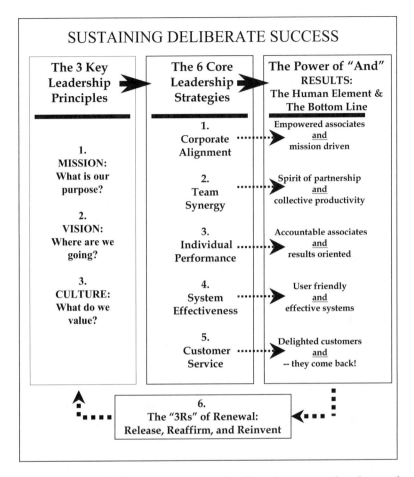

SUSTAINING DELIBERATE SUCCESS

Reinvent. In this journey to organizational mastery, leaders celebrate successes, take corrective action, and continue to reinforce purpose, passion, and performance.

Each of the **6 Core Leadership Strategies** contributes individually and collectively to the effectiveness of a successful, self-renewing organization by emphasizing performance results on both The Bottom Line *and* The Human Element.

1.   **Corporate Alignment:** This strategy focuses on the "big picture" of leadership responsibility to build

ownership of and commitment to the overall purpose and direction of the organization. Leaders need to actively engage and empower people at every level, from Board members to the newly hired, in supporting the mission and values.

Desired Performance Results:

- Finance and operations reflect the corporate principles and values, and
- Empowered associates are inspired by the mission and vision.

2. **Team Synergy:** This strategy focuses on the necessity to create sustained benefits from the collective and creative energy of the "wild geese flying in formation." While honoring differences, leaders align talent in service to the mission and vision.

Desired Performance Results:

- Goal accomplishment is greater than the sum of the parts, and
- A climate of partnership, trust, and service prevails between and within individuals and teams.

3. **Individual Performance:** This strategy focuses on attracting, retaining, coaching, and developing individuals to use their talents and gifts at the highest level. Like at Southwest Airlines, you "hire for attitude and train for skill." Peak-performing organizations "go for gold" in hiring the best then continue to invest in the development of people to assure maximum utilization of human potential.

Desired Performance Results:

- Individuals demonstrate high quality and productivity in serving the "big picture," and
- Principle-centered, accountable associates function as stewards of organizational resources.

4. **System Effectiveness:** Financial, human resource, computer, and a host of other support systems link the various organizational components together to facilitate achieving and sustaining high outcomes.
   Desired Performance Results:
   - Systems need to support and enhance operations, and
   - These same systems must be user friendly, simple, and responsive.

5. **Customer Service:** Whether internal stakeholders or external customers, leaders are challenged to create a culture that thinks, breathes, and practices customer service in its highest form.
   Desired Performance Results:
   - Customers need to experience high value at a fair cost, and
   - By "delighting" our customers, they become our advocates. Fulfilled employees and delighted customers build business.

6. **The "3 R's" of Renewal:** This element emphasizes a deliberate and ongoing effort to **release** practices and behaviors that no longer serve the company, **reaffirm** that which continues to benefit the company, and to **reinvent** individuals, teams, products and services to assure a cutting edge position in this competitive market.

Ongoing feedback from the first five Core Leadership Strategies enables an organization to actively challenge every strategic and tactical activity to stretch to higher levels of performance. This self-assessment and feedback process, however, requires safety to make "hamburger out of the sacred cows" and courage to make the tough decisions. Self assessment and organizational renewal brings the feedback loop right back to **The 3 Key Leadership Principles**:

1. Mission: What is our purpose?
2. Vision: Where are we going?
3. Culture: What do we value?

Individuals and organizations that sleepwalk through life set themselves up for certain demise. Imagine how beneficial application of the "3 R's" would have been to IBM and Polaroid at key points in their history in releasing their sacred cows and reinventing themselves. Deliberate Success, on the other hand, results from planning a course of action, working that plan, getting key factor feedback, and self-correcting. Deliberate Success begins and ends with emphasis on **The 3 Key Leadership Principles** that direct and shape an organization: Mission, Vision, and Culture.

"Apple was in a coma a few years ago, but we're back to innovation again."

—Steve Jobs, CEO, as quoted in *Newsweek*, July 31, 2000

These **3 Key Leadership Principles** come into sharp focus when planning, prioritizing, and problem solving. At every choice point, ask: *Is what I am doing right now bringing us closer to or further from our purpose, our direction, and our values?* The decisions you make shape your future; decide wisely.

the decision diamond: a test of mission, vision and culture

Courageous leaders venture into uncomfortable and often unpredictable territory to do that which is right in moving closer to what they seek. Significant decisions need to be principle-centered and value-based—regardless of the circumstances.

the decision diamond

To what extent is this decision:
- Aligning with our mission?
- Bringing us closer to our vision?
- Honoring our values?
- Supporting our strategies
- Emphasizing our priorities?
- Serving our key stakeholders?

Courageously resist succumbing to political pressure or to short-term expediency. Both what you decide and how you go about making that decision communicates critical messages about what is really important in your corporate culture.

"Though no one can go back and make a brand new start, anyone can start from now and make a brand new ending."

—Carl Bard

"Walking your talk" is a moment-by-moment application of decisions and actions that reflects your mission, brings you closer to your vision, and honors your values. Pay careful attention to each decision point and what messages your choices are sending to stakeholders both within and outside of the organization. Making principled decisions consistent with what you profess to be important builds stakeholder clarity, confidence, and commitment in the renewal process.

deliberate success gem

Leadership: Shaping Your Future

Contributed by Alex Trotman

For starters, know your stuff. Study hard at your chosen profession. Master the skills. Today's working world is an intensely competitive place, and knowledge is the basic price of admission.

Think and compete globally. Markets, capital, technology, information, and products increasingly ignore national borders. You need to learn about other cultures: how they think, how they communicate, how they do business. A second language is good; a third better.

Be flexible, but durable. The world is changing; don't let it change without you. The ability to learn, adapt, and absorb the inevitable failures is key to staying in the race.

Know how to lead. Leadership is more than "authority"; it's courage, vision, ethics, and grounding in reality as well. Think about leadership. Read about it. Study it in the leaders you respect. It's important.

And remember: None of this works without determination. Success is not for the ambivalent. It's for those who know what they want and go after it, no matter how difficult the path.

—Alex Trotman
Former Chairman and CEO,
Ford Motor Company
www.ford.com

Holding yourself accountable to make principled decisions role models integrity in action. The real test of your values occurs not when things are going well; the real test occurs when things are not going well. How you function under adverse conditions, how you function when it really counts, and how you function when leading your organization through periods of significant change all communicate vital messages to the critical stakeholders. By linking what you do with what you say, trust develops and stakeholders are more likely to move from resistance to commitment.

As a leader, your job is to give voice to your vision and to courageously facilitate the process of deliberately shaping your future. Your ability to master the art of renewal and build enthusiastic supporters separates the good leader from the great leader.

"The only sustainable advantage comes from out-innovating the competition."

—Tom Peters

chapter 16

keep your fire burning

> "Passion is something that starts in the gut, floods the imagination, and comes to reside in the will. Passion is disciplined when it has focus, consistency, persistence, and, above all, integrity."
>
> **—James Kouzer and Berry Posner**

SOME REFER TO it as "fire in the belly" and still others claim it's the "Gung Ho!" attitude. Whatever it's called, leaders must develop, instill, and nurture that sense of passion and commitment to sustain high levels of performance—in themselves and in others. Passion cannot be forced through external means; it results from a patient and persistent cultural application of the principles and tools described throughout this book.

You experience that "Pride in Performance" when you have a tire changed at Les Schwab Tire Service in the Pacific Northwest. You can take delight on a festive flight with Southwest Airlines. You can revel in the spirit of service with "on-stage" employees at Disneyland. None of these experiences are accidental; they result from a deliberate, long-term leadership commitment to creating giants out of their employees and providing services that delights their customers. It's not only these peak-performing corporations that can teach us about instilling passion. Consider what we can learn from a "primitive" tribe:

With fascination, I watched a Discovery Channel documentary about a primitive tribe recently discovered by anthropologists deep in the rain forest of a South American jungle. Although the tribe depended upon fire to cook their food, they did not know how to make fire! How could this be? Many generations ago, their ancestors originally learned to cook from a fire apparently started by lightening. The tribe charged one person with the responsibility of keeping the fire burning, the "Fire-Keeper." This legacy then passed on with great honor— generation after generation—to the most respected member of the tribe. Entrusted with sustaining the very lives of the tribe, the "Fire-Keeper" has the awesome responsibility of keeping the fire burning in a rain forest. If the fire were ever to go out, the tribe itself would perish.

Sustaining the corporate spirit deserves as much attention and commitment as does the Fire-Keeper's exalted responsibility to maintain the eternal flame in a rain forest. Every organization needs a Fire-Keeper to create a compelling vision, ignite the spirit, release the talent, and generate the passion to convert the mission into reality. As a leader, that's your job: to be the Fire-Keeper. With a compelling mission and vision, people will join you in cocreating impressive results. Sustaining that purpose, passion, and performance remains a challenge for leaders. How are you sustaining the magic? How are you keeping the "fire burning" in your personal life and in your business?

Ruthita Fike, a hospital CEO client I have consulted with for a decade, is one of the most brilliant role models of a corporate Fire-Keeper that I have experienced. As a visionary leader who engages and empowers people, she demonstrates long-term effectiveness in aligning The Human Element and The Bottom Line. Her commitment to both people and productivity creates an environment that focuses on purpose, instills passion, and results in high levels of performance. How does she do that? She deliberately "tends the fire" in four specific ways.

In one of a number of executive development sessions I facilitated, her team identified four leadership commitments to which they wanted to hold themselves accountable:

- Fire-Keeper.
- People-Builder.
- Servant-Leader.
- Operations Master.

Not just words on a piece of paper, the executive team clarified behavioral expectations, identified implementation strategies, and determined methods of measuring progress for each of the four leadership commitments. The process itself reinforced their values while positioning the executive team to function at an even higher level of performance. Notice that with the four leadership commitments, Ruthita, in close consultation with her team, first created a *dream, decided* to act, *developed* methods for keeping the "fire burning," then *delivered* results.

> "We cannot be a source of strength unless we nurture our own strength."
>
> —M. Scott Peck

1. **Fire-Keeper:** Developing and nurturing a healing environment for patients and staff requires leaders who honor that same spirit within themselves. Each member of the executive team willfully accepted the fire-keeping challenge with a high level of awareness and keen sense of commitment. They fully comprehended the significant value of keeping the corporate flame burning in spite of obstacles.

2. **People-Builder:** This commitment reinforces the benefit of hiring and developing winners. Not leaving it up to chance, Ruthita Fike is an accomplished talent scout who relentlessly pursues top-quality people to join her team. Once on board, she and her associates continue to coach and develop all levels of associates in the hospital. Even as the CEO, she makes herself readily available for coaching feedback by her associates as part of her ongoing personal and professional development.

3. **Servant-Leader:** This next commitment reinforces the responsibility to be principle-centered and value-driven with each decision and with each action. The servant-leader emphasizes releasing and empowering rather than directing and controlling as people work synergistically to convert the vision into reality.

4. **Operations Master:** Bottom-line results count, and this final commitment focuses on attaining and sustaining outstanding financial, productivity, technical,

and quality targets from an operational perspective. Peak-performing organizations achieve significantly enhanced results because talented people are empowered to give their very best in service to shared vision and values. People take seriously their stewardship responsibilities in using corporate assets wisely and with integrity.

Deliberate Success requires that you and your team integrate the principles of being a fire-keeper, people-builder, servant-leader, and operational master. Either you work your own agenda or you will be working on someone else's agenda. It's that simple in this competitive business economy—and in life.

"The illiterate of the future will not be the person who cannot read. It will be the person who does not know how to learn."

—Alvin Toffler

Wise leaders invest in the ongoing development of themselves, their associates, their products, and their services to continually sharpen their competitive edge. As knowledge and technology become rapidly obsolete, you have options about the extent to which you allow yourself to fall behind or move ahead. Keeping your fire burning brightly reflects the extent to which you are willing to both create favorable change and adapt to changes imposed by customers, competitors, technology, and the economy. You are in charge of your own personal and professional renewal program—of keeping your fire burning even though you might be in a "corporate rain forest."

Leaders need to be masters of change, and they simultaneously need to maintain strong allegiance to the "roots" that support and sustain greatness—namely mission, vision, and values. At every choice point along the way, leaders and associates alike ask, "Is what I am doing right now bringing us closer to or further from our purpose, our direction, and our values?"

Shaping change, rather than reacting to it, positions you and your business for a more successful and rewarding future. Individuals, teams, products, and services need to be in a constant state of reinvention and renewal. The effective leader, then, becomes a futurist, a visionary, a strategist, a talent scout, a coach, a cheerleader, and, perhaps most importantly, a fire-keeper.

"You must live in the present,
launch yourself on every wave, find your eternity in each moment."

—Henry David Thoreau

---

deliberate success: just do it!

Success is not an accident. Success in life and in business results from deliberate and consistent efforts to achieve desired results. In spite of the **5 Success Strategies** and scores of implementation tools explored in *Deliberate Success*, some people still might ask: Well, how do I apply this? How do I put it into action? How do I bring out the best of my team? How do I create success in my own life?

"SUCCESS - To laugh often and much; to win the respect of intelligent people and affection of children; to earn the appreciation of honest critics and endure the betrayal of false friends; to appreciate beauty, to find the best in others; to leave the world a bit better, whether by a healthy child, a garden patch or a redeemed social condition; to know even one life has breathed easier because you have lived. This is to have succeeded."

—Ralph Waldo Emerson

You already know what you need to know and you already know what you need to do. Trust in yourself; the answers are within. Rather than postponing action or procrastinating, it's time to perform. It's a matter of just doing it! Nike's corporate motto ("Just do it") inspires action in spite of obstacles. Are you prepared to act on what will create more success in your life—in spite of the obstacles?

> "If you want to know your future, look at what you are doing in this moment."
>
> **Tibetan saying**

Peter Block, author of Stewardship and The Empowered Manager, wrote the

 ## deliberate success gem

"How? Just Do It!"

Contributed by Peter Block, Ph.D.

I was with a group that wanted to know how to implement empowerment and employee participation. Who doesn't? I asked the audience how many of them had read the books *Thriving on Chaos*, *Seven Habits of Highly Effective People*, *The Empowered Manager*, and *The Fifth Discipline*. Most of the group raised their hand. Those four books contain more than 925 specific suggestions on how to achieve higher performance and enhanced customer service. So if we have read those books and others, and if there are more practical suggestions than we can use in a lifetime, why are we still asking the question "how?"

The question "how?—more than any other question—looks for answers outside of us. "How?" is an indirect expression of our doubts, a defense against taking action. Asking this question, when we already know the answer, keeps us stuck in inaction and leads us to conclude that we need more information, more support, more encouragement, and more resources. We immobilize ourselves by this self-defeating process.

If we took responsibility for our freedom, committed ourselves to service, and had faith

(cont.)

(cont. from p. 273) that our security lay within ourselves, we could stop asking "how?" We would see that we have the answer. In every case, the answer to the question "how?" is yes! The solution resides within the person asking the question.

Instead, ask these questions:

1. What will it take for me to claim my own freedom and create the experience of my own choosing?
2. When will I choose to use my talents in service to self and others rather than to hold back and settle for?
3. When will I finally choose adventure and accept the fact that there is no safe path?

Saying "yes" to questions of freedom, service, and adventure—as an individual and as a work unit—opens up the possibility of beginning our own experiment in partnership and stewardship. It takes only one diet to lose weight, it takes only one instant to stop smoking, and it takes only one decision to which we commit to make a difference. We know how. We have only to decide and have the courage to live with the consequences.

—Peter Block, Ph.D.
Author of *Stewardship* and
The Empowered Manager
www.peterblock.com

adjacent "Deliberate Success Gem" for inclusion in this book. How might his message apply to you?

"You are the only one who can do your part."

—Kris King

What you seek in life is usually only a decision away. Your business and personal success starts with a vision and results from the deliberate actions you have the courage to implement. Dream big. Keep the fire burning. And let your actions send a resounding "yes!" to realizing your vision.

"Be the change you want to see in the world."

—Mahatma Gandhi

endnotes

DELIBERATE SUCCESS: REALIZING Your Vision with Purpose, Passion, and Performance represents a compilation of best practice principles and tools gathered over more than two decades of consulting experience. Additionally, my ideas were influenced by the many talented authors and consultants who committed their "best stuff" to writing in the following treasure chest of resource books and audiotapes. Throughout *Deliberate Success,* I have referenced a number of authors through endnotes that correspond to their work identified here.

1. Freiberg, Kevin, and Jackie Freiberg. *Nuts!,* Austin, Texas: Bard Press, 1996.
2. Phillips, Donald T. *Lincoln on Leadership*. New York: Warner Books, 1992.
3. Nanus, Burt. *Visionary Leadership.* San Francisco: Jossey-Bass, Inc. 1992.
4. Drucker, Peter F. "Really Reinventing Government," *The Atlantic Monthly,* February 1995, pp. 49–61.

5. Collins, James C., and Jerry I. Porras. *Built To Last.* New York: HarperBusiness, 1994.
6. Ibid.
7. Freiberg, Kevin, and Jackie Freiberg. *Nuts!,* Austin, Texas: Bard Press, 1996.
8. Blake, Robert, and Jane Mouton. *Consultation.* Reading, Penna.: Addison-Wesley, 1976.
9. Allenbaugh, Eric. *Wake-Up Calls: You Don't Have To Sleepwalk Through Your Life, Love, or Career.* New York: Simon & Schuster, 1994.
10. Collins, James C., and Jerry I. Porras. *Built To Last.* New York: HarperBusiness, 1994.
11. Ibid.
12. Desatnick, Robert L. *Managing to Keep the Customer.* San Francisco: Jossey-Bass, 1987.
13. Albrecht, Karl and Ron Zemke. *Service America,* Homewood: Dow Jones-Irwin, 1985.
14. Block, Peter. *Stewardship: Choosing Service Over Self-Interest.* San Francisco: Berrett-Koehler, 1993.
15. Freiberg, Kevin, and Jackie Freiberg. *Nuts!,* Austin, Texas: Bard Press, 1996.
16. Collins, James C., and Jerry I. Porras. *Built To Last.* New York: HarperBusiness, 1994.
17. Scott, Cynthia, and Dennis Jaffe. *Empowerment: Building A Committed Workplace.* Los Altos: Crisp Publications, 1991.
18. Keyser, John S. "Beyond Management to Leadership," in *Toward Mastery Leadership In Student Development Services.* The American Testing Program, 1986.
19. Buckingham, Marcus, and Curt Coffman. *First, Break All the Rules: What the World's Greatest Managers Do Differently.* New York: Simon &

Schuster, 1999.

20. Block, Peter. *Stewardship: Choosing Service Over Self-Interest.* San Francisco: Berrett-Koehler, 1993.

21. Senge, Peter M. *The Fifth Discipline.* New York: Doubleday, 1990.

22. Allenbaugh, Eric. *Wake-Up Calls: You Don't Have To Sleepwalk Through Your Life, Love, or Career.* New York: Simon & Schuster, 1994.

23. Collins, James C., and Jerry I. Porras. *Built To Last.* New York: HarperBusiness, 1994.

24. Buckingham, Marcus, and Curt Coffman. *First, Break All the Rules: What the World's Greatest Managers Do Differently.* New York: Simon & Schuster, 1999.

25. Ibid.

26. Allenbaugh, Eric. *Wake-Up Calls: You Don't Have To Sleepwalk Through Your Life, Love, or Career.* New York: Simon & Schuster, 1994.

27. Ibid.

28. Kriegel, Robert and Louis Patler, *If It Ain't Broke...Break It!,* New York: Warner Books, 1991.

select bibliography

Albrecht, Karl and Ron Zemke, *Service America,* Homewood: Dow Jones-Irwin, 1985.

Allenbaugh, Eric. *Wake-Up Calls: You Don't Have To Sleepwalk Through Your Life, Love, or Career.* New York: Simon & Schuster, 1994.

Ankarlo, Loren and Jennifer Callaway. *Implementing Self-Directed Work Teams.* Bolder: CareerTrack, 1994.

Blake, Robert, and Jane Mouton. *Consultation.* Reading: Addison-Wesley, 1976.

Blanchard, Kenneth, and Michael O'Connor. *Managing By Values,* Escondido: Blanchard Training and Development, 1995.

Blanchard, Kenneth. *Mission Possible: Becoming a World-Class Organization While There's Still Time.* New York: McGraw-Hill, 1997.

Block, Peter. *The Empowered Manager: Positive Political Skills at Work.* San Francisco: Jossey-Bass, 1987.

Block, Peter. *Stewardship: Choosing Service Over Self-Interest*. San Francisco: Berrett-Koehler, 1993.

Buckingham, Marcus, and Curt Coffman. *First, Break All the Rules: What the World's Greatest Managers Do Differently*. New York: Simon & Schuster, 1999.

Collins, James C., and Jerry I. Porras, *Built To Last*: New York: HarperBusiness, 1994.

Covey, Stephen R., Roger Merrill, and Rebecca Merrill. *First Things First*. New York: Simon & Schuster, 1994.

Crosby, Robert P., *Walking the Empowerment Tightrope: Balancing Management Authority & Employee Influence*. King of Prussia: Organization Design and Development, 1992.

Desatnick, Robert L. *Managing to Keep the Customer*. San Francisco: Jossey-Bass, 1987.

Drucker, Peter F. "Really Reinventing Government," *The Atlantic Monthly*. February, 1995, pp. 49-61.

Freiberg, Kevin, and Jackie Freiberg, *Nuts!*, Austin: Bard Press, 1996.

Garfield, Charles. *Peak Performers: The New Heroes of American Business*. New York: William Morrow, 1986.

Geraghty, Barbara. *Visionary Selling: How To Get To Top Executives — And How To Sell Them When You're There*. New York: Simon & Schuster, 1998.

Giber, David, and Louis Carter, and Marshall Goldsmith. *Linkage Inc.'s Best Practices in Leadership Development Handbook*, San Francisco: Jossey-Bass Pfeiffer, 2000.

Keyser, John S. "Beyond Management to Leadership," in *Toward Mastery Leadership In Student Development Services*. The American Testing Program, 1986.

Kriegel, Robert and Louis Patler, *If It Ain't Broke...Break It!*, New York: Warner Books, 1991.

Marriott, J.W., and Kathi Ann Brown. *The Spirit To Serve: Marriott's Way.* New York: HarperBusiness, 1997.

Nanus, Burt. *Visionary Leadership.* San Francisco: Jossey-Bass, Inc. 1992.

Patterson, Kerry, and Joseph Grenny, Ron McMillan, Al Switzler. *The Balancing Act: Mastering the Competing Demands of Leadership.* Cincinnati: Thomson Executive Press, 1996.

Peters, Tom, and Nancy Austin. *A Passion for Excellence.* New York: Random House, 1985.

Peters, Tom. *The Circle of Innovation.* New York: Alfred A. Knopf, 1998.

Phillips, Donald T. *Lincoln On Leadership.* New York: Warner Books, 1992.

Schutz, Will. *The Human Element.* Muir Beach: Will Schutz Associates, 1980.

Scott, Cynthia, and Dennis Jaffe. *Empowerment: Building A Committed Workplace.* Los Altos: Crisp Publications, 1991.

Senge, Peter M. *The Fifth Discipline.* New York: Doubleday, 1990.

Tracy, Brian. "Reinventing Your Business," *Insight,* No. 151, Chicago: Nightingale-Conant, 1995.

Waitley, Denis E. *The Psychology of Winning.* Chicago: Nightingale-Conant, (Audiotape) 1988.

Wall, Steve and Harvey Arden. *Wisdomkeepers: Meetings With Native American Spiritual Elders.* Hillsboro: Beyond Words Publishing, 1990.

index

about the author

DR. ERIC ALLENBAUGH is a national and international consultant who focuses on creating and sustaining individual, team, and corporate excellence. Additionally, he is a seasoned executive coach and sought-after keynote speaker, having addressed in excess of 1,500 audiences in more than 40 states. He has had two major careers: a dozen years in hospital administration and now more than two decades as a leadership consultant in peak performance.

He authored the popular book *Wake-Up Calls: You Don't Have To Sleepwalk Through Your Life, Love, or Career* (published in hardcover by Bard Press in 1992 and in paperback by Simon & Schuster in 1994). Additionally, he has authored a number of other leadership resource booklets and magazine articles on creating and sustaining individual and team excellence.

Eric resides with his wife, Kay, in Lake Oswego, Oregon. Kay is the author of the best-selling series of inspirational books for women titled *Chocolate for a Woman's Soul.*

To find out more about how Dr. Eric Allenbaugh can support your commitment to individual, team, and organizational success, contact:

Allenbaugh Associates, Inc.
Lake Oswego, Oregon
www.allenbaugh.com